Sylvia tried not to stare at him...

What a hunk! she thought. But just wait until he heard her proposal. "Look, Craig, I'm not interested in marriage, but I would like to have an affair." She hastened to add, "That is—I want to *pretend* to have an affair. My plan is that you would pretend to be my lover for the week you're here, and my family will be so relieved when you leave that they'll leave me alone." She smiled mischievously, and her green eyes sparkled at him.

"You want me to pretend we're having an affair?" he asked incredulously. A flicker of interest darkened his eyes. He reached across the table to take her hand and began to caress it.

"Let's not get carried away. It's only pretend," she replied nervously.

"Of course. Shall we start now?"

Dear Reader,

Welcome to Silhouette. Experience the magic of the wonderful world where two people fall in love. Meet heroines who will make you cheer for their happiness, and heroes (be they the boy next door or a handsome, mysterious stranger) who will win your heart. Silhouette Romances reflect the magic of love—sweeping you away with books that will make you laugh and cry, heartwarming, poignant stories that will move you time and time again.

In the next few months, we're publishing romances by many of your all-time favorites, such as Diana Palmer, Brittany Young, Emilie Richards and Arlene James. Your response to these authors and other authors of Silhouette Romances has served as a touchstone for us, and we're pleased to bring you more books with Silhouette's distinctive medley of charm, wit and—above all—*romance*.

I hope you enjoy this book and the many stories to come. Experience the magic!

Sincerely,

Tara Hughes
Senior Editor
Silhouette Books

SUE SANTORE
A Man for Sylvia

Silhouette Romance

Published by Silhouette Books New York

America's Publisher of Contemporary Romance

This book is dedicated to Diana Palmer.
Many thanks, Diana, for all your advice and encouragement and the inspiration of all those wonderful books.

SILHOUETTE BOOKS
300 E. 42nd St., New York, N.Y. 10017

ISBN: 0-373-08480-3

First Silhouette Books printing January 1987

America's Publisher of Contemporary Romance

Printed in the U.S.A.

SUE SANTORE

has traveled and lived in several states and now lives with her husband of twelve years and their three children in the lovely state of Maine. Sue loves to read and write romances and is a firm believer in "happily ever after." Sue and her husband were pen-pals and decided to get married two weeks after their first meeting—just like something right out of a romance novel.

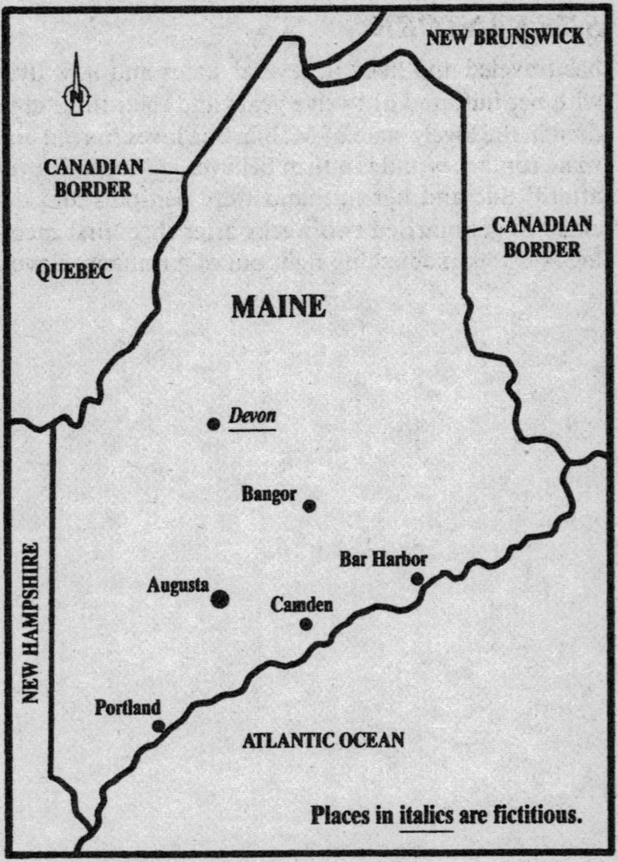
NEW BRUNSWICK
CANADIAN BORDER
CANADIAN BORDER
QUEBEC
MAINE
Devon
Bangor
NEW HAMPSHIRE
Bar Harbor
Augusta
Camden
Portland
ATLANTIC OCEAN
Places in italics are fictitious.

Chapter One

Sylvia Perkins carefully eased her new car into the narrow garage and turned off the engine. She smiled up at her waiting brother.

Jody leaned on the shiny finish of the car. "Where did you steal this, Sylvia?"

"Very funny." She frowned at him. "This is my birthday present to myself."

"Nice. Very nice." Jody glanced at the soft upholstery and sleek dash panel. "But a red Thunderbird?"

"I've waited long enough for it. You know how many times a week you had to jump start my old car last winter."

"A new battery wouldn't cost ten thousand dollars."

"How much would a new brother cost?"

"Don't say that in front of Carol. She might write you out a contract."

"Are you having problems again?"

Jody ran his fingers through his thick hair. "You could say that. Mostly it's that the kids came too fast and I don't make enough money." Little worry lines that Sylvia had never noticed before were etched around Jody's eyes.

"What about your computer repair sideline?"

"There aren't enough people here in Devon with computers that need repair. There aren't enough people in Maine for Carol, period. And not enough money to open a computer store to sell more computers to repair."

Sylvia sighed and climbed out of the car. Jody was her only brother, her favorite sibling, her mirror image, and she hated seeing him like this. He was two years younger than she, and he looked at least two years older. Since the arrival of their third child last month, he and his wife, Carol, had been having serious financial problems, which led to lots of fights about everything unimportant.

"You know I'd give you money."

"I know. But you've worked hard for what you've got and deserve to keep it." They walked to the side door leading into the kitchen, and Jody opened it. His green eyes looked tired, and he ruffled his red-brown hair with a restless hand. "If I can't support my family, you can't afford to support it."

"Grandma should have left this house to you and Carol instead of me." They entered the roomy kitchen, and Sylvia dropped her handbag and a stack of school papers onto the large pine table. "It's really too big for me." Was she trying to convince Jody or herself? She looked around the room that held so many memories. Childhood treasures. Adult suffering. The rest of the old house, built in 1847, was elegant and tastefully decorated. This room was simply comfortable.

Jody shook his head. "You deserved it. You quit your teaching job to stay with her and took complete care of her for two years so she wouldn't have to go to a nursing home. Grandma knew what she was doing."

Remembering how alert she had been right up until that last evening, Sylvia had to agree. "I'm glad you said that because I really love this house. I'd hate to leave it, but sometimes I feel so guilty about being the one to have it. Everyone else has a family but me."

"Speaking of which—"

"Not you too, Jody."

"Aunt Willy, not me. She insists on my getting you a date for the joint birthday party she's giving you and Momma next Saturday night."

Sylvia grabbed up the stack of school papers and whacked them down against the tabletop. "If I have to listen to one more lecture on hitting thirty without being married, I shall scream!" She glared at Jody. "Aren't there enough grandkids, nieces and nephews around without everyone getting on my back about finding a man and having my own? Maybe I like being alone!"

Jody held up his hands in protest. "Hey—you know I don't care. I'm just the messenger. Course she did want the message delivered differently."

"I just bet she did." Sylvia paced the floor in the roomy kitchen with long strides. "It would serve them right if I had an affair." Her thick mahogany hair bounced against her shoulders as she turned sharply and strode back past Jody.

A wide grin spread across his face, as he leaned indolently against the wall, his hands shoved into his pockets. "An affair? Oh, Sylvia, that's rich. Mom would call a family conference and Aunt Willy would marshal Father O'Neal for backup."

Sylvia stopped and glared at him, then a tiny smile crept out of her tightly held mouth. "That's true, they would." Her green eyes glinted mischievously. She stared out the window at the row of stately old homes across the street as the smile curved and spread. "I'll do it," she spoke in a quiet, decisive manner.

"Are you serious?" Jody straightened and stared at his attractive sister. "The first night a strange car parked in your garage, it'd be all over town."

As though she hadn't heard him, Sylvia pulled out a chair from the table and sat down, reaching for a scrap of paper and a pencil. "Let's see. Number one. There's Mr. Turner, the school janitor. He's single."

"He's also sixty and bald."

"Number two. Jimmy Frilby, works in the bank. He's asked me for a date several times."

"He's been divorced three times, he's a foot shorter than you and he's ugly as homemade soap."

"Number three. Mark Lord, the high school principal. He's tall and good-looking."

"Even worse. He's married."

"Jody, this is an affair. Married doesn't count."

"Don't be ridiculous, Sylvia. If you want to seriously convince anyone that you, of all people, are having an affair, it has to be someone worthy of you."

"How archaic you sound. 'Someone worthy of you.'"

"Well, you are special. You're my favorite sister and darn good-looking, too."

"Why, thank you, Jody." Sylvia was touched. Compliments weren't thrown around much in her family. She doodled slowly on the list she'd made before looking up at her brother. "There's Harold. I could always write him that Grandma is dead."

"That creep? He dropped you quick enough when you took on her nursing care, and never even told you when he left for Boston and greener pastures. He left that to his mother."

The pencil snapped. Sylvia abruptly stood up. "Let's face it, Jody. My social life is the pits, but that's all going to change."

"Just like that?" Jody gave her an incredulous look.

"Just like that," she repeated firmly. "Now why don't you go home? I have a lot of papers to grade tonight so I can get my reports in. You know school ends in a few weeks. And I have to buy Mom's birthday present tomorrow."

"I don't know if I dare leave you now. You might drag some unsuspecting tourist in off the street. The poor man wouldn't have a chance."

Sylvia knew he was only half joking. It was common knowledge in her family that when she made up her mind to do something, she did it, regardless of the opinion of her family or neighbors. Many people had told her that she was wasting years of her life taking care of Grandma, that she should put her in a nursing home, but Sylvia had remembered all the times that Grandma had been there when they were kids, and she had ignored all the advice and admonitions, going ahead with what she thought was the right thing to do.

"Promise me you won't do anything foolish."

"Am I in the habit of doing foolish things?"

"No, but—"

"Then hush, and go home."

Jody hesitated, shrugged and started toward the door. With his hand on the glass knob, he turned back toward Sylvia. His sister stood almost equal to him in height, her statuesque figure perfectly proportioned. Red highlights shimmered in her hair from the late afternoon sun shining through the tall bay window. "Oh, Sylvia, one thing."

"Yes?"

"Look in the mirror sometime besides just to comb your hair."

"What's that supposed to mean?" Sylvia yelled after him as he escaped out the side door into the garage. The sound of the heavy garage door sliding up and down obscured any answer Jody might have given. In exasperation, she watched him amble across her lawn to his old truck. The engine choked and gasped before sputtering with halfhearted chugging noises as Jody jerked down the street in the rusty beast.

Sylvia turned back to her pile of papers and sighed. Feeling mild hunger pangs, she rummaged in the refrigerator and came up with a carton of cottage cheese. She dug into the drawer for a fork and tucked herself into a chair in front of the schoolwork. Eating a forkful of the soft stuff, she started pricking the pages with her red pen, causing the makeshift efforts of her students to bleed.

Soon her pen slowed and stopped, and she said aloud, "So, Sylvia. To celebrate your thirtieth birthday, you're going to have an affair. With whom?" She tapped the table with her pen. That was the problem. Fingering the diamond earrings, another gift from Grandma that she had had reset for her pierced ears, Sylvia sighed and shoved the papers aside. "A minor technicality, my dear." She mimicked her Aunt Willy's voice. "After all, you have a week to find someone." Maybe I could advertise in the classifieds, she thought. *Woman wants affair. Apply quickly.* She smiled at her silliness.

Grading papers appealed to her even less than usual tonight. She did no more work, watching mindless comedies on television to pass the evening and retiring early, only to lie staring into the darkness, listening to the friendly creaking of the old house.

Tossing about on her bed, she remembered the scene when she'd told Harold about her decision to nurse Grandma and that they'd have to postpone their marriage. He'd resented her loss of income even before he could place his hands on it. That had been the last night she'd seen him. His mother had called her a week later with the news of his exit to Boston. Talk about getting desperate, Sylvia told herself. I must be, to even think about calling him.

Why can't they leave me alone? I'm happy. I have a lovely old house filled with genuine antiques, a new car all paid for, a steady job. Why must I have a man too? She punched her pillow in irritation at her nagging relatives. And I don't need help to get a date, she countered perversely. Finally her body overcame her mind and she fell asleep.

Since it was Friday night, she had made certain the alarm was turned off and it was comfortably late the next morning when she awakened. After a quick breakfast, Sylvia dressed in gray slacks, a softly tucked gray blouse and a pin-striped blazer. A coral necklace and her green eyes and mahogany hair were her only colors. A quick look in the mirror confirmed that everything was in place and she was ready to browse for a suitably gross gift for her mother. She smiled affectionately at the memory of the gaudy, overdecorated gifts her mother loved.

After digging out her car keys from the caverns of her purse, she pulled the garage door up with one swift swing, halting its upward flight at the very tip of its runners. Turning back to her car, she marveled at the shiny newness of it once again. And it was hers. All hers. Not even partly the bank's. As she drove along the roads to the small shopping center on the edge of town, enjoying the smooth ride and unfamiliar luxury, a roadside setup caught her eye.

A dull red pickup with the tailgate hanging down over the license plate was parked beside the entrance to the shopping center. On the grass beside the truck, dozens of garish velvet paintings were displayed. Two cars had stopped and the people were browsing among the framed pictures.

Just the thing for Mother's birthday present! Sylvia decided. She slowed the car and parked along the curb. Sauntering between the display rows, she ignored the reproductions of rock stars and movie idols and found a section of animal pictures. A small painting of two kittens gamboling together attracted her attention. Mother will love this, she thought. Picking up the picture, Sylvia carried it over to the heavyset man standing near the truck, in front of a table with an old cash register. A crumpled hat was pulled low over his head, placing his face in shadows. Creepy old man, Sylvia thought.

"I'd like to buy this picture, please." The man twisted his hat, grunted and rang up the purchase, handed Sylvia the change from her fifty and turned away. She took the dirty bills gingerly. He certainly wasn't very friendly. Wondering where he was from, Sylvia attempted to initiate polite conversation. "This is for my mother's birthday present."

The man's back stiffened. He turned and bent close to Sylvia, his eyes glittering from the shadows of his hat. In a strange rote voice, he asked her, "When is her birthday?"

"Next Saturday." Curious. Maybe he knows Mom, she thought.

"Then you don't want this one," was the cryptic reply. Taking the painting from Sylvia, the man climbed into the rear of the truck.

Sylvia waited for a few minutes, then she frowned and looked at her watch. What was he doing? Her foot began to tap impatiently. This had better not be one of those come-ons where she didn't get the picture after she'd paid for it. Just as she was wondering if she should call the cops, he returned with an exact replica of the one she had chosen.

"This is the one you want."

"Thanks." I guess, she thought. "It looks the same."

A crooked smile broke the straight mouth of the man into a twist, highlighting a scar etched across his cheek. "I expected—your brother?"

A puzzled line wrinkled her forehead. "He's busy today."

"I heard it's nice this time of year out on old Barlow Road."

What was he talking about? "Sure," she said. With a slight shrug, she dismissed the subtle changes in the man's behavior and left with her mother's gift. Placing it carefully on the front seat beside her, she drove around the corner of the tiny shopping center to park in front of Smiths department store.

She didn't see the man standing in the vestibule of the Smiths store, standing where he had a good view of the truck and paintings on the lawn, down the road a short distance. She didn't see him, but he sure saw her. His eyes narrowed and he stepped back as she came through the door. What a looker she was! He hadn't expected Freddy to have this kind of contact. And she carried that ugly painting with her as if she didn't dare part with it.

Thinking about her scheme to foil her relatives' attempts to push men at her, Sylvia had abstractedly tucked the picture under her arm when she slid out of the car. She wandered over the sidewalk and into the store. As she started down an aisle, a young girl at the service desk called to her, "Oh, ma'am. You have to check your parcel before shopping here."

Check my parcel? What parcel? She glanced down and saw that she had the painting under her arm. Now why did I bring this in here? Then, not wanting to check her mother's gift, she refused. "No. I don't want to check it."

"You have to check it," the flustered girl repeated.

"Why? You don't sell these here."

"It's the store policy."

Sylvia tilted her chin stubbornly. "Then I won't buy anything here." She sensed a male shadow looming over her and turned to stare him in the eye, only to find herself looking up at the biggest man she had ever seen. He was even taller and broader than her dad. "And I don't care if you're the new manager. It's a dumb policy and I'm leaving." She strode toward the door, clutching the painting tightly.

"I agree with you." The deep voice rumbled next to her ear as she spun out the door. "It is a dumb policy when obviously they have nothing of that quality in the store."

Sylvia jerked her head around to look at him. Was he making fun of her present? She eyed him suspiciously. "You aren't the manager? Who are you?"

Smooth black hair was casually styled and set off his dark eyes and square jaw. A tiny scar curved across the slight hump in his nose. His massive shoulders stretched the fabric of the beige knit shirt and the tan corduroys fitted over the thickest pair of muscled thighs Sylvia had ever laid eyes on. I bet he has to order his shoes custom-made, she thought irreverently.

"May I see your picture?" A massive hand reached out and deftly removed the painting from under Sylvia's arm. He turned it around to look at her selection. "A very nice choice. Are you hanging it in your apartment?"

Although Sylvia was aghast at his taste in art, the sheer attractiveness of the man appealed to her. Perfect. Just perfect, she thought. Wouldn't Aunt Willy and Momma die if I showed up with this handsome monster?

"No. Anyway, I don't have an apartment," she said as she took back the painting. "I have a house."

"Really? With lots of lovely children playing in the backyard behind a picket fence?"

"No."

"No children? Or no picket fence?"

He certainly was persistent. "No to both. I'm not married." Now why had she told him that? Would he think she was fishing?

"Then no one would have any objections to your lunching with me at John's Pizza?"

"No one—unless I did." Sylvia tossed her hair back and slid her gaze along his magnificent frame again, ending at his face. He was perfectly still, yet she retained an impression of energy in motion from the intensity of his eyes.

"And do you?" he asked in a husky voice.

How can anyone make a simple three-word sentence sound sexy? Sylvia wondered. *Sylvia, if you throw this golden opportunity away, I'll never forgive you.* She smiled up at him, one shy dimple peeking out at him briefly. "None at all. Just let me store this painting in my car."

They walked past the row of cars in the parking lot until Sylvia came to her Thunderbird. She decided to unlock the trunk and tuck the painting in it for safe-keeping, although why anyone would want such a monstrosity was beyond her. Picking up an old blanket that she had laid in the trunk to keep the carpeting clean, she wrapped the picture to prevent it being scratched, and pushed it into the rear of the trunk.

"Nice car." He glanced at the dealer's tag still on it. "Brand-new?"

"Yes. I just bought it yesterday," Sylvia answered proudly as they threaded their way back through the maze of cars to the sidewalk and John's Pizza. She realized that he had never answered her question about who he was. When he reached out to grasp her elbow to steer her around a cluster of chattering teenagers, perceptive eyes observed them and a giggling chorus of "Hello, Miz Perkins," followed them.

Preoccupied by the tingle that assailed her arm in the warm grasp of his hand, Sylvia absently smiled at her kids and waved, then turned her attention back to her lunch partner. "I'm Sylvia Perkins." She waited expectantly. Silence. "And you are?"

"The name is Craig. Craig McDonald."

"I've never seen you before. Have you been in town long, Craig? What do you do?"

"Here we are," Craig spoke in his deep voice that fit his huge body perfectly. He placed his hand on the small of her back, steering her quickly through the door into the spicy aroma of homemade pizza.

"Hello, Sylvia. What can I do for you today?" John bustled up from the rear of the store. "I'll take their order, Mike," he told his assistant.

Sylvia could feel the searching curiosity as John eagerly waited for some explanation of her appearance with a strange man. She was determined not to give him any. This is all my business, she thought. Nobody else's.

"Do you like pepperoni and anchovy?" she asked out loud.

Craig nodded.

"One pepperoni and anchovy, John, and two Cokes." She laid down half the money for the pizza as John made out a slip for them. Craig silently tossed a matching five-dollar bill onto the counter. Quickly Sylvia led Craig to a lonely table in the rear of the brightly painted restaurant. As they sat down, she apologized, "I hope you don't mind my hurry. We were about to get the third degree."

A muscle rippled in Craig's cheek and was still. He bent over the table to speak to her. "May I ask why?"

With a little sigh, Sylvia said, "Because you're with me." He might as well know it now. "Over half the town knows me and will be intensely curious about you. Everyone wants me to get married, but I'm perfectly happy just as I am, thank you."

Craig raised his heavy eyebrows. "So, you're trying to tell me that if I'm seen with you, I pique the interests of everyone in town."

"Yes," she reluctantly agreed.

"Is that good or bad?"

"Good if you're a traveling salesman. Bad if you're an undercover cop."

"An undercover cop. My, you have a lively imagination. Why not an innocent tourist?"

"Are you in town for long?"

A hint of reserve crept into his voice. "Until I get some business taken care of. Maybe a week or so."

"Aha. Tourists don't take care of business." She threw him a triumphant look. *A week*. More and more perfect. The tiny hint of an idea that had nudged her outside of the Smiths store was now growing and forming. "So tell me about yourself, Craig. What's a nice guy like you doing in a little town like Devon?"

A chuckle rumbled deep in his chest. "Isn't that my line, Sylvia? And I could add—what's Freddy the Hat to you?"

"Freddy the what?" She gave him a confused look. "What *are* you talking about?"

"Never mind." Craig shifted his bulk in the small chair, trying vainly to get comfortable. He smiled across the table at Sylvia, his black eyes fathoms deep. "Just my little joke."

"Weird." She grimaced at him, then smiled back. It was nice sitting across the table chatting with Craig. She sensed something dangerous about him, but she'd have been willing to swear the danger was not to her. Her emotional impressions of people were rarely wrong. She had even known Harold was a jerk before he'd disappeared out of her life, but that had been while she'd been brainwashed into thinking a jerk was better than no man at all. Craig was definitely not a jerk. The vague plan began to take definite shape in Sylvia's fertile mind.

"What state are you from?"

"What makes you so sure I'm not from here?"

"Come on."

"Most recently, New York. I was born in Ohio about thirty-five years ago." With an amused glance at her he continued. "I'm single. I shower every day. I squeeze the toothpaste in the middle and I like mountain climbing. Anything else important for you to know?"

Sylvia nervously shredded the paper from the plastic straw. Did she dare ask him? Then a vision of Aunt Willy's pointing finger rose up before her. *You need a good man, girl. Why don't you get married-married-married?* The smoldering resentment at the constant jabs she'd been forced to endure seethed up and gave her courage.

Looking swiftly around to make sure no one could overhear them, she leaned forward eagerly. "I want you to know that I'm not interested in marriage."

"You said that. Thanks for the reassurance—I think." He grinned at her, which softened his firm chin and eased the impression of guardedness.

"Look, Craig," Sylvia explained further, "I'm not interested in marriage, but I would like to have an affair."

A flicker of interest darkened his eyes even more.

She hastened to add, "That is—I want to pretend to have an affair. You see, I have four siblings all younger than me, all married with lots of babies. My sisters all want poor Sylvia to find a man and settle down like them. And so do my mother and one of my aunts. They're driving me crazy." She tapped her fingers on the table for emphasis and leaned forward conspiratorially. "My plan is that you would pretend to be my lover for the week you're here and they'll be so relieved to see you go that they'll leave me alone." She smiled mischievously and her green eyes sparkled at him.

"You want me to pretend we're having an affair?"

"That's right." Sylvia beamed at him as though he were one of her slower students who had finally grasped the difference between a noun and a verb.

Craig reached across the table and engulfed her hand. He gave her an odd smile. "We'd have to hold hands in public for people to believe we're lovers." He caressed her hand.

His hand was warm and gentle and completely covered hers. *Nice. I could get used to this,* Sylvia thought.

"And, I'd have to put my arms around you, and kiss you, and taste your mouth with mine, and caress you, and touch you in front of everyone."

Her mouth dropped open. A warm glow spread through her at the unexpected thought of Craig's arms cradling her and his mouth exploring her own. She had considered the theory but not the practice. Glancing away from him she agreed, "Um, I guess some of that would be necessary."

"Oh, definitely necessary."

"But let's not get carried away. It's only pretend."

"Of course. Shall we start now?"

"Now?"

"Here comes your friend with our pizza. Shall we impress him?"

May as well start now, she thought, then I'll get used to it by the time I confront my family. "Sure, why not?"

Chapter Two

John's eyes widened as he neared their table with the hot pizza. Sylvia knew that the sight of her holding hands across the table with a good-looking stranger was frontline gossip, and that John's wife would never forgive him if he didn't call her right away.

So it was no surprise to Sylvia that as he placed the box on the table, he made a hurried departure to the back of the building. She chuckled. "He's off to make a phone call. By evening my mother will call me to find out what's going on."

"Are you serious?"

"Oh, yes. News travels fast in a small town where most people know each other."

A thoughtful look crossed his face and Sylvia wondered if he was regretful about their agreement already.

"News travels fast, huh? So most of the town will know I'm here by morning."

"'Fraid so. Want to back out of our game?"

"Definitely not. This promises to be one of the most interesting assignments I've had."

"What work do you do?"

"Oh, I travel around a lot here and there," he replied vaguely. "What do you do?"

"I'm an English teacher."

"Is that how you know everyone?"

"That and the fact that I grew up here, mostly. My dad was in the air force but we were always moving, so we spent all our vacations here with our grandparents. It was nice to have someplace permanent. Then when he retired we came here to stay. I was fourteen."

Craig asked Sylvia question after question while they shared the large pizza. The unfamiliar attention of a very attractive man went to her head like a third glass of wine to a teetotaler's. She talked freely to him about everything. Everything except Grandma. Somehow she couldn't mention her long nursing role or the unexpected legacy that Grandma had left her. He might misunderstand, maybe think she was bragging.

After the pizza was devastated, Sylvia remembered her overdue grocery shopping; she had to have some food in the house. "I have to stop at the A&P, Craig. Want to go with me? We can pretend we're shopping together. Part of the plan."

He grinned at her. "I'm beginning to like this plan more and more. Do I get to help eat part of it?"

Sylvia shifted uneasily. "I don't think dinner at my house would contribute any to our affair unless someone from my family comes."

"We could pretend it's a rehearsal."

"You're not taking this seriously, are you?" She frowned at him.

"I couldn't be more serious."

Suddenly she had a brief, intense vision of what a real affair would be like with Craig. Sweet heaven! What a fatal mistake that would be. For a moment she wondered if Jody would consider him "worthy" enough, then decided she didn't care. All she knew was that she had never met anyone half as sexy as Craig McDonald. And probably never would again, she admitted to herself.

"We'd better go now." Sylvia was proud of herself. Her voice didn't shake at all and her hands trembled only slightly. She'd have to eliminate these disturbing thoughts before Craig suspected the source of her agitation. And, oh, what a source.

The source stood up and towered over the table. Sylvia slid out of her seat and, straightening up to her five feet, eleven inches, looked up at him. "Just how tall are you?"

"Are you implying I'm too big?"

"You're not just big, you're mammoth."

"Thanks a lot."

"You're welcome. And I like mammoths." She was amused by the pained look that marred his face. "In case you hadn't noticed, I'm not exactly petite."

The sweeping search Craig gave her—from the smooth tips of her shoes up the gray slacks to the coral necklace, and ending with an intense look into her green eyes—would have made Sylvia blush if she'd had any blushes left. But she'd lost them all long ago and she felt only uncomfortable.

Grasping her elbow, Craig steered her toward the door. "Didn't anyone ever tell you that you are one good-looking hunk of a woman?"

Now it was Sylvia's turn to wince. "Don't you know women are supposed to be beautiful, or adorable, or at least cute? They are not, I repeat *not*, supposed to be hunks." This was said while she was gently being shoved out the door by Craig's hand, which felt like a small shovel on her spine.

As she turned to glower up at him, he flashed her one of those quick grins and slithered his hand up her back, catching the back of her neck. "I like hunkie women."

Her knees felt curiously liquid and her hand lifted and fell back without completing its mission. She stared at him a moment, then turned to march to her car, followed closely by Craig.

Warm fingertips closed over her hand as she reached for the door on the driver's side. "Let me drive."

"No deal. I just bought this car and I'm driving it." Sylvia was adamant. The big lug might be her answer to family pressure, but she'd be darned if he would drive her brand-new car.

Craig capitulated gracefully and climbed in beside her. "I should be thankful for small favors."

"Such as?"

"That you're tall enough to drive with the seat all the way back. My mother crumples my knees under the dash." He crossed his arms and stretched out his legs comfortably.

"Your mother?"

"Don't sound so surprised. I didn't spring forth from Zeus's head."

"It's hard for me to picture you as a little boy. Were you naughty?"

"Of course not!" His liquid velvet eyes slashed sideways toward her. "Unless you count blowing up the chicken house with a homemade bomb...with the chickens in it."

"With the chickens in it?" Sylvia gave a strangled gasp. "Why?" She turned the corner at the square and drove down the street toward the small A&P.

"My brother was the leader of the other side and they were holed up in the chicken house," Craig admitted with a slightly guilty look.

"Oh, no. You were never naughty. Did your parents kill you?"

"I got some hard whacks on my seat with the back of my mother's hairbrush. But what about you? With green devil eyes like that, you must have been bad."

"Not me," Sylvia denied as she slid the car into a wide parking space. "I was a darling child."

"Sylvia—" Craig turned to her with a undefinable pattern on his face "—anyone who thinks up a scheme like this to confound her matchmaking relations is no newcomer to madcap doings."

"Pooh. You're just jealous I thought of it."

He grinned—wide and wolfish. She never could explain later exactly how he did it, but she suddenly found herself scooped out from under the steering wheel and resting nicely on his lap.

"For heaven's sake, Craig. Someone will see us," she hissed at him, ignoring how enjoyable it was to be held against his massive frame. *Bro-ther!* Jimmy Johnston was standing on the corner with his pals, and his mother was on the school board! "Craig, let me up!"

"You're just jealous I thought of it." His mouth was only millimeters away from hers. "I'm going to kiss you Sylvia. Right in front of your whole town."

"Craig, we just met."

"Don't you remember?" His arm snaked up and welded her to him. "We're having an affair."

"Just...pretend." She managed to allow the words to escape her lips.

"Right. We're practicing pretending." His steady black eyes caught her green ones. The inky depths fascinated her, so like the silken black hair and the crisp dark curls at his opened buttons. When his mouth caught hers she forgot about Jimmy Johnston and his mother.

Craig tasted her delicately, deliberately, his mouth possessing hers in a warm, slow motion.

Sylvia slipped forward against Craig as his mouth left hers and wandered across her face. As he tasted each closed eyelid and nuzzled behind her ears, she felt her temperature rise at least ten degrees. With her eyes still closed, her voice finally spoke in spite of her body telling it to shut up. "It's getting late. We'd better get the food and get it home before the troops start looking for me."

"Troops?" Craig's voice had a peculiar thick sound as he reluctantly opened his door and bounced Sylvia off of his lap.

"My family. Most Saturday nights we visit back and forth. Sundays we all attend mass together and take turns putting on dinner." She knew she was babbling, but didn't care as they entered the safe neutral zone of the brightly lit A&P.

Craig stared at her intently. A green-eyed sexy amazon who was a school teacher, went to mass regularly and talked intimately with Freddy the Hat? What kind of family was it? A Maine Mafia? He'd have to meet more of her relatives. A wide smile spread across his face. "I'll go to mass with you tomorrow."

Sylvia shook her head. "No, no, no. If I were having an affair, I wouldn't go to church."

"Why?"

"It's out of character," she retorted smugly.

"Okay. While you're staying home because of your sins, let me help you with dinner and tomorrow can be your turn."

A single tingle of anticipation trickled up her spine and disappeared as she clamped onto her defense system. One week. Just pretend, she reminded herself. "It has been several weeks since everyone came to my house," Sylvia said, while thinking that it might be a good idea to introduce him before the birthday party. The affair would appear to be more real than if she just showed up with him once. "All right, Craig McDonald. But you show up tomorrow at twelve-thirty. I don't need any help with dinner."

Craig agreed and they spent the next half hour strolling the store and piling her cart high with groceries. "For a woman living alone, you sure must eat," was his brief comment when she threw three chickens, a roast, and a two large packs of pork chops into the basket on top of the seven steaks.

"I have a lot of company." Sylvia wondered about the strange look he gave her.

Pushing the heavy cart, Craig stopped before a display of popcorn. "Popcorn. Do you have popcorn?"

"I don't know if I've any left or not. Why?"

"I love it." He threw three bags of yellow popping corn into the loaded cart.

"What'd you do that for?"

"Don't you know one of the rules of an affair is to feed your lover his favorite food?"

"You're easy to please," she said as she headed for the cashier.

An intense gleam flashed in his eyes. "Oh, very easy."

Sylvia ignored his subtle hint and concentrated on lifting out the food to place it on the checkout counter.

"Sylvia! How nice to see you today." The young cashier, MaryLou, glanced sideways at Craig and back at Sylvia. Her eyes glistened with curiosity. "I see you have a helper today."

"Yes." Sylvia was noncommittal.

"Relative...or friend?" Her finger hesitated above the keyboard.

With a sigh, Sylvia replied. "He's a friend, MaryLou, and no more questions, please. Just check me out."

Did she hear a ghostly whisper, "I'd like to check you out"? Turning, she frowned at Craig. His dark eyes stared back innocently at her. How could he manage to look sexy and so darn innocent?

After riding home with her and helping her put away the groceries, Craig declined her offer of a lift back to his car, saying he'd rather walk. She watched him go down the sidewalk with long strides. He moved swiftly and was soon out of sight.

Only then did it sink in that she had actually suggested to a total stranger that they have an affair. The logical side of her brain nitpicked. "I didn't ask him to have an affair, only to pretend to have one." But the other side of her brain was appalled and told her, "You must be a real nut, Sylvia." And then the slow realization dawned on her that although Craig had learned a great deal about her, she knew absolutely nothing about him, except that he wasn't going to be around long.

A fleeting thought crossed her mind that maybe he was casing her house for a robbery. No. She rarely ever made a mistake judging character. And she had had only good feelings about Craig—and what good feelings!—except she had the impression that he was holding back something.

She couldn't say the same for that guy at the truck with the pictures. He had given her the creeps. I wouldn't want to meet him on the proverbial dark night, Sylvia thought. She wondered where he was from. Maybe from West Devon? Or he might be from anywhere, just passing through. Aunt Willy might know; maybe she'd ask her tomorrow.

Tomorrow. She had scads of cooking to do before her locusts descended tomorrow. While searching through her collection of cookbooks for a special menu, Sylvia stopped to wonder why she was going to so much trouble for just another family dinner. The answer was, it wasn't just another family dinner.

At this dinner she would present her alleged affair to them. They'd be horrified. Chuckling softly to herself, Sylvia imagined the various reactions to her pretended relationship with Craig. Then he'd be gone next week, and she'd tell them some story about it not working out. They'd be so glad that she wasn't sinning anymore that they'd finally leave her alone. A pleased smile widened her mouth as she finished writing out her recipe selection and stuck the paper under the ceramic cookie jar.

Since it was a bit chilly, Sylvia decided to start the old wood stove in the kitchen rather than stoke up the furnace. She pushed the button to start the automatic trap door opening and the wood elevator rising, until the woodbox had clicked into place beside the stove. What the family had considered Grandma's extravance had come in handy when she was dying of cancer. Sylvia had been able to feed the stove without descending into the basement and leaving Gran alone in the little room next to the kitchen that they had turned into her bedroom.

After grabbing an old newspaper off the top of the stack she had brought down from the attic the week before, Sylvia crumpled up several sheets and stuck them in the stove, carefully placing small pieces of kindling on top. Lighting a match to the paper, she watched the curl of flame grow and lap at the wood as her thoughts drifted. She did love this house. The old embossed metal ceilings, the decorative wood moldings, the large rambling rooms. It was too bad it couldn't be filled with children.

Sylvia shrugged. What man would be able to stand her large outspoken family? Look at how fast Harold had escaped, using Grandma's illness as an excuse. Anyway, she told herself as she shut the stove door and rose to her feet, I am happy, just as I reminded Jody. I have a good job, friends, a loving family. What more could I need? A smiling male face popped into her thoughts. Craig? Good heavens, no, Sylvia, she told herself. A mammoth is definitely not what you need.

Calling her mother to volunteer to host Sunday dinner, Sylvia braced herself for the onslaught of questions she would surely receive as a result of the gossip chain. Not a single interrogative word came from her mother's lips. Merely pleasant agreement and that she'd pass the word along. Very strange, Sylvia mused as she hung up the phone.

On Sunday Sylvia rose early, determined to have the perfect dinner ready for the slaughter of the innocent. Only they weren't so innocent. All of them had been badgering her for years. They deserved the whole charade.

As she bustled around the kitchen chopping, mixing and stirring, the doorbell rang. Sylvia wiped her hands and headed for the front door. Passing through the living room, she glanced at the huge grandfather clock in the corner opposite the fireplace. Ten-thirty. *This had better not be Craig.* She didn't want him there without her noisy crowd. Pretending to have an affair was one thing. Actually having one was another. She couldn't handle a series of short-term sex hops and she knew it. That's why she usually steered clear of dating. Most men saw Sylvia as a hot-to-trot single, especially the blind dates Jody occasionally made for her at her aunt's pressing.

She swung open the hand-carved door, smoothing the wood polished by many hands for many years. A tall, slender man dressed in an expensive-looking suit and carrying a briefcase stood on her front porch. His features were picture perfect. Blond hair rolled to one side, definitely styled, not just a haircut. A classic nose. Features that could have been molded from clay. An old saying of her mother's flicked into her head. *A pretty man always knows it. A handsome man never does.*

"And what can I do for you?"

A perfect smile flashed at her and she remembered Craig's crooked grins.

"Good morning, madam. Are you the lady of the house?"

"Yes, I am." She folded her arms and spaced her legs apart. "You have five minutes for your sales pitch, because I'm very busy."

"Oh, no, ma'am. I'm not selling anything. I'm taking a consumer survey and I'd just like to ask you a few questions. May I come in?"

Sylvia hesitated, then opened the door. "Just for a few minutes. I really am busy."

Another perfect-teeth smile. He slid in the door behind Sylvia. When she turned to shut the door and turned back, he was already on the couch with his briefcase opened on his knees.

"You move fast." Sylvia raised her eyebrows at him.

"Don't want to waste your time." He wagged a finger at her. "Now if you'll just sit down, Mrs....?"

"Just Sylvia, please."

"I'm Roy Pratty." He pulled out a sheet of paper and began to ask her questions about how she shopped and what brands she bought. Then the questions became more personal. Job? Income? Family? "Of course I'll understand if you don't wish to answer any of these questions," he told her.

Sylvia answered all his questions without hesitation. "What company are you doing this survey for?" she asked him, curious as to why he was in this small town. "Does it pay to send out survey takers to little towns?"

"Only to a selected few. Devon, of course, having such a good reputation."

"Devon? You've got to be kidding! I didn't think anyone outside of a fifty-mile radius had even heard of Devon, Maine."

"Oh, yes. My dad even lived here years ago."

"Really? What was his name?"

"Um, Jed... Jed Pratty."

"So you're a Mainiac?"

"No, I was born after he moved away." Roy Pratty, survey taker, leaned back and looked at Sylvia out of those big blue eyes. "Say, I have to stay in town for a few days. How's about going out with me tomorrow night to have a pizza? We could talk about people Dad knew back when."

Two men in two days. Things are looking up, Sylvia, she told herself. Why not? she thought, remembering her last pizza. Craig certainly wouldn't care. "That would be nice," she said.

"Fine." The smile of a model rested on Roy Pratty's face. "I'll pick you up at six."

No sooner had Sylvia seen Roy to the door and made it back to the kitchen to pick up a set of measuring spoons than the doorbell rang again. "Darn it, I'm never going to get this food fixed." She threw down the spoons and marched back to the door. Throwing it open, she scowled up into Craig McDonald's crooked grin. Dressed in a sleek three-piece suit, he looked good enough to have for dinner. Pretty Roy paled beside his harsh masculine handsomeness. "You're early," she accused him and shoved the door shut against his quickly inserted foot.

"You're nice on Sunday mornings."

"And I don't want you here with me alone."

"Why not? We're having an affair."

Sylvia narrowed her eyes at him through the slit in the door. "Pretending. Don't get your hopes up."

"Did I hear you end a sentence with a preposition? And you an English teacher. Tsk. Tsk."

"Oh, shut up." The man had the ultimate skill for changing the subject. She yanked the door open.

"Since you're here, I guess you can come in, but watch it."

"I'll be glad to—if you'll tell me what it is."

"No more kisses."

Craig tilted his head and gave her a steady stare from his midnight-black eyes. "You didn't like my kiss?"

Shifting uneasily under his waiting gaze, Sylvia wondered what to say next. She glanced around the kitchen seeking a simple solution and found none, so she took a deep breath and faced him. "Your kiss was fantastic and you know it, but I'm not the hop-in-bed-and-run type. You're only going to be here a week and you kindly agreed to play a game with me to help me out. That's all there is."

He shoved his hands into his pockets and answered, "It's your game, Sylvia. You call the shots."

"How can I," she blurted angrily, "when you stand there looking better than any man I've ever met?"

A startled look rippled Craig's composure then vanished, leaving an inordinately pleased expression. "Really? Do you really think so?"

All Sylvia could think about was the pleased expression on her grandfather's Saint Bernard when, as a child, she had patted him on the head for retrieving a stick. She sighed. "Come on, you big lug. You can mash the potatoes."

"I'm a whiz with potatoes."

"I certainly hope so."

It was strange, the smooth way they worked together in the kitchen, as if they anticipated each others needs and moves. In a surprisingly short time dinner was ready and waiting, including a gooey German chocolate cake for dessert.

It was twelve noon. The inquisitors would be arriving any minute. As Sylvia glanced from the immaculate table settings to the buffet groaning with food, she realized what fun it had been working with Craig. Too bad he isn't going to be around longer, she found herself thinking as she glanced over at his large hands refilling the ice trays with water. I could get used to him fast. . . .

A few minutes later the first victims arrived: Jody and Carol.

"Wait here a minute," Sylvia commanded Craig. She dashed to the front door to intercept Jody.

While Carol took the baby upstairs to change him, Sylvia pounced on her brother. "Jody, I found him."

"Who?" was his absentminded answer as he corralled his two toddlers.

"You know, my affair."

Jody stiffened and turned to face Sylvia. "You *are* joking."

"No, he's in the kitchen. I want you to meet him before the horde gets here. Jody—wait!"

Jody hit the kitchen door on the run, kicking it open and slamming it back in Sylvia's face.

"Come on, kids." She scooped up the two squirming youngsters and pushed open the swinging door with her bottom. The sight of Jody and Craig eyeing each other and circling like two bantam roosters—no, scratch that, two very large roosters—met her amused sight.

"Will you simmer down, Jody? This is Craig McDonald—and Jody, my brother," she explained to Craig. Dropping the children, she grabbed Jody's arm and tried to shake him. "Craig has agreed to *pretend* with me that we are having an affair, so everyone will get off my back. Haven't you, Craig?" She turned to him for confirmation only to find him staring at her and Jody with a peculiar openmouthed expression on his face.

"What's wrong?" she asked in alarm, then realized before he spoke that she and Jody were standing side by side and were both wearing gray suits with pale blue shirts. His slightly greater height and her longer hair and feminine figure were the only physical differences between them.

"Did you clone yourself while you were gone?" Craig's gaze returned to Sylvia then moved back to Jody.

Sylvia chuckled as the open mouth gradually closed. "We used to fool the family all the time. When we were kids, I was such a tomboy that Momma cut my hair short so she wouldn't have to fight the tangles." Sylvia looked up at Craig as she continued her story. "One day she looked right at me and called me Jody and told me to take out the garbage. She was so upset that she made me wear pink ribbons in my hair until it grew out again." She chuckled at the memory. "Remember, Jody?"

Looking up at Jody's disturbed expression, she jabbed him in the side with her elbow. "Jody, knock it off. For Pete's sake, I'm almost thirty years old. I can take care of myself."

"I doubt it." He gave Craig a defiant look. "McDonald? You sure don't look like a hamburger patty—more like a huge slab of beef."

"Jody!" Sylvia was appalled at his rudeness. Just as she turned to apologize to Craig, she heard more car doors slamming outside.

Chapter Three

Sylvia grabbed Craig's tightly muscled arm and nudged him. "Come on, we have to start the show." She was so intent on watching the herd trooping up the sidewalk to her front door that she missed the intense look Craig gave her as she snuggled against his side.

Sylvia smiled serenely as her family avidly stared at Craig and his encircling arm. The buzzing gossip sped around the large living room as it filled with people of all ages. Momma marched up to the two of them, followed closely by Aunt Willy, demands pasted across their faces. Defusing their questions, Sylvia said in a loud voice, "Hi, everyone. I want you to meet Craig McDonald. He's in town on business and—we're having an affair."

Silence pressed into the room. Horrified faces swiveled as if on a string to stare at Sylvia and Craig.

She chortled inside at their reactions, even as the warmth of Craig's arm soaked into her ribs. It's really too bad this is all pretend, she thought.

Ignoring the shocked expressions of her conservative family, Sylvia led the way into the formal dining room adjoining the living room and kitchen. A tiny part of her mind registered the fact that her father had a small pleased smile on his face, and she wondered how much of the truth he had guessed. He had always been the one to catch their switches when she and Jody had succeeded in fooling everyone else, but she knew he wouldn't tell on her.

The anxious faces had blurred together for Craig. It wasn't until after they had sat down at the table for dinner that he could pick out individual members to whom he had been introduced. He received the distinct impression, from the looks of most of Sylvia's relatives, that he was about as welcome as a hungry raccoon in a chicken coop.

For some reason he wanted to tell them that there was no affair, that it was only a game. He was sure they would have been pleased if Sylvia had announced that they were getting married. Married! He must have rocks in his head. He had thought it a great idea to pretend to have an affair—to slide into a real one while he was working on this latest job. Sylvia was one sexy lady, just his size. So what was the problem? The problem was that she wasn't his usual type of bedtime date. She was the permanent type. White picket fence, two-point-five children.

And he still didn't know where she came into the picture. She didn't seem like a criminal accomplice.

And when she brushed up against his arm and smiled at him like that, he almost didn't care if she was. She was one gutsy woman. If she wanted to convince them that he was her lover, he'd be a real heel to let her down, now wouldn't he?

When Craig returned the smile and nudge with which she had anxiously sought his attention, Sylvia was filled with a vast relief. For one moment she had seen hesitation on his face and wondered if he was backing out. Her family was a bit much for an outsider to handle, even if he wasn't going to be around long.

Slowly Craig's fingertips slid across her shoulders and lightly rubbed her opposite cheek, turning her head gently as he leaned over to brush his lips across her face and whisper in her ear, "How'm I doin'?"

"Great. Just great. Keep it up," she whispered back to him with a soft smile—entirely for the benefit of the family, of course. She steadfastly ignored the delicate shivering sensation beginning to spread wider and wider at his easy touches, and concentrated on how wonderful it would be to have the family off her back about marriage after this short term "affair." Why, all she'd have to do would be to threaten to have another one.

The dinner was eaten in strained silence, broken only by her father's cheerful comments to Sylvia and Craig, and their equally cheerful replies. Jody glowered at them both all through the meal. Her sisters cast covetous looks at Craig and horrified glances at Sylvia. Momma and her usually voluble sister-in-law ate in shocked silence, jumping up occasionally to wait on the noisy children who were eating at card tables in the corner of the room.

After the meal, when the halfhearted offers to help with the dishes were met with Sylvia's swift comment, "Oh, no. Craig and I will do them," the crowd left hastily with stilted goodbyes. Sylvia smiled serenely at all of them and ignored a careful wink from her father as he hugged her and gave Craig a firm handshake.

When all the cars and trucks with their stunned occupants had disappeared, Sylvia turned to Craig and threw her arms around him to give him a quick hug. "We did it! Thanks Craig, I..." Her words trailed off as she looked up at him from such an intimate position, becoming aware of the solid feel of his chest and the tight muscles of his thighs pressing against her thin slacks. Quickly she dropped her arms and started to step back only to find herself enclosed within his powerful embrace.

"I have a better thanks in mind."

As Sylvia watched his mouth descend slowly, ever so slowly, she told herself, I can handle another kiss. Nothing to it. Then his mouth landed and her soft response was swallowed up as the flames that still flickered low within her from his first kiss flared up. She was burning inside with a welcome heat that was spreading insidiously, uncontrollably. With gentle pressure Craig tasted her thoroughly, his arms wrapped around her body, his legs firmly holding her in place.

This kiss was as advanced from that first tentative touch as a volcano from a Fourth of July sparkler, and

Sylvia began to feel like molten lava as the heat spread through her body and turned her blood to liquid fire. Seeping through her veins, the fiery warmth softened her and she relaxed into his embrace, twisting her hips against him, instinctively seeking to find the ultimate source that could both fuel the blaze and quench it.

One last thread of sanity held Sylvia to the untamed devil inside her that whispered, *Nothing to it? Just a kiss? Now you've done it, Sylvia. Just because you're coming up thirty doesn't mean you have the right to take out your frustrations on an innocent bystander.* The words of her little devil penetrated the wealth of newly discovered sensations, and Sylvia recognized in dismay that she was acting like one of her randy teenage students.

"Craig— No!" Pushing hard against him—trying to convince herself as much as him—Sylvia managed to get her "stop" message across. As the encircling arms loosened around her, she stepped back. Hot jade-green eyes locked with smoked midnight-black.

As they looked at each other, their eyes saw what their lips would not speak about. Sylvia's mahogany hair was tangled from the interplay of Craig's hands and her unsteady breathing and shaking arms gave a lie to the calm manner in which she leaned over the table to begin stacking dishes.

Drawing a few deep breaths himself, Craig passed his hand over his face. What was the matter with him? It was just another kiss with an attractive woman, after all. *Just another kiss? That's what you'd like to think—but you know better.* He did know better. That was the trouble. He couldn't afford to get seriously involved with any woman, not with his job, and definitely not with this woman. This wasn't turning out at all the way he'd planned. Not at all.

"Maybe you'd better leave now, Craig." Sylvia straightened from the stack of plates and platter of silverware. Keeping a distance between them, she looked straight at him and didn't try to hide her feelings under a joke. "This is getting out of hand."

"I know." He didn't pretend to misunderstand. What had started out a game had ended up something entirely different. He still wasn't sure just what. Shaking his head uneasily, Craig said, "It isn't what I'd planned either."

"Just what had you planned?" A curious detachment separated her from his honest words.

"I'd planned on seducing you."

"And what happened?"

"Darned if I know!" He ran in fingers through his hair in a gesture of frustration. "I was having fun—then wham-o!"

A small smile tugged at the corner of her mouth. "My sentiments exactly. That's why I think you should leave now."

She followed him to the door in silence. When he turned to leave and would have spoken, Sylvia held up one finger and wagged it at him. "Uh, uh. No regrets, no goodbyes. Thanks for your help fooling the folks. Now just go."

After shutting the door behind him, she locked it, something she rarely did. Something usually unnecessary in her protective neighborhood. What was she really trying to lock out? She leaned against the locked door with her head tilted up and eyes closed. "Well, Grandma. The fat's in the fire. Can you hear it sizzling?" She slapped herself on the cheek. "Cut it out, Miz Perkins. Tomorrow is a school day and you have dishes to wash and papers to grade."

Work was always good for curing thinking. While Sylvia cleaned up the many dishes from the dining room and the innumerable pots and pans in the kitchen, she steadfastly refused to consider the ridiculous pact she had made with Craig. After the first outraged phone call from a relative, she took the telephone off the hook, and diligently attempted to correct the stack of personal essays from her students, trying to find something encouraging to write on each one.

When the grandfather clock in the living room struck ten, Sylvia shoved the unfinished papers aside. Standing up, she pulled down the rolltop on her desk tucked into the corner of the warm kitchen, stretched and sighed and left the room. Opening the door that concealed the old servants' stairs, she slowly stepped upward. At the top of the stairs was a concealed door that led into the hall near the room that had once belonged to the maid.

Swinging the door shut behind her, Sylvia wandered down the hall toward the refinished bathroom. After a quick bath, she wrapped herself in a thirsty blue towel, then went in search of her favorite flannel nightgown when she couldn't find it in her drawer. She finally found it in the hall linen closet.

Shaking her head at the mental collapse that hovered over her as she neared that fatal birthday, Sylvia drew back the covers on her antique brass bed and crawled into sanctuary. But sleep fled her as thoughts of her reactions to Craig's casual touches and two kisses could not be delayed any longer. Lying perfectly still on her back, staring up into the darkness, Sylvia Perkins had to face the fact that she wanted a virtual stranger to make love to her.

Feelings had been stirred in her that she had forgotten since that fumbling time with Harold, after which she had decided that she was destined to be an old maid, as Aunt Willy insisted on calling it. But these feelings were far fiercer than those old longings. *You were very close to being out of control,* her devil rose up to chide her. *Miz Perkins, English teacher, even at thirty, you're not ready for this!*

Furious at the prodding demon, she sat up in bed. "I'll show you. Here I come, thirty or not!" She punched her pillow and lay back down, wondering why she couldn't have met Pretty Boy first and used him for her "affair." She was sure that there would have been no melting fires with him. That word struck her and she sat up again. *Used.* She had been trying to use Craig for her own personal needs, without considering his needs at all.

Shame for her stubborn stupidness lumped in her throat. As she remembered the hard warmth of his body, her bed felt empty for the first time in ages and she wondered if having a real affair would be such a bad idea. After all, she had the name, why not the game? And Momma and Aunt Willy kept telling her that she was almost "over the hill."

Slumping back onto her pillow she fell asleep with jumbled dreams of tall skinny men with pretty faces all chasing her up a hill, while she searched for her own gentle giant.

The shrilling of the alarm clock the next morning jarred Sylvia from her bed. She forced herself to get ready for school and made up her mind that no matter what gossip was floating around she would treat the day as a usual one on the job.

That resolution lasted until she arrived at the teachers' lounge to drink her second cup of coffee. The buzz of voices hushed as she entered the room and swung her briefcase on top of the pile on the floor beside the small stove. Mareen Towne, from the business department, swished over to stand by the stove.

In a sickeningly sweet voice she asked, "Is it true, Sylvia? Do tell us it isn't."

Sylvia carefully poured the hot coffee into her mug. Tossing back her hair, she looked steadily at Mareen. "Why? Did you want to give me some pointers first?"

A titter ran around the room and Mareen sucked in her breath. "Then it is true."

Sylvia glanced around the room at the various expressions on the faces of her colleagues, ranging from sympathy to eager curiosity to downright glee. Her stubborn Perkins blood came to her rescue and she tilted up her chin, plucked her briefcase out of the pile and, tucking it under her arm, turned to go. Before she went out the door, she paused and turned back, glancing around the room again, then fixed Mareen with glacier cold green eyes.

"I don't care whether you think it's true or not. My private life is just that." And she left the room, brushing past the early students in the hallway without seeing them.

Her cheeks flushed with anger, she strode down the hall to her senior homeroom and inwardly groaned when the first student to walk in the door was Jimmy Johnston. He was the class leader and when he made no comment she was relieved, only to notice that all the kids were coming in quietly and sitting quietly, too quietly, since the bell hadn't rung yet. Sylvia was wondering just what they had heard when the bell rang. The last straggler dashed in and Jimmy Johnston raised his hand.

Silently sighing, Sylvia asked, "Yes, Jimmy?"

Jimmy stood up and gave a cool look around the room before hitching his thumbs in his jeans pockets and looking back at Sylvia. "We just want you ta know, Miz Perkins, that you're the best English teacher we ever had. And we don't give a—" With an effort he swallowed his expletive. "We don't care what the gossip is. And it's not gonna matter to the other kids, either. We'll see to that." As his speech ended, he sat down with a proud smile on his face.

As Sylvia looked around at the other seniors in her room, she was touched. The dozen other large boys nodded in agreement with Jimmy. And her pseudo-sophisticated group of girls gave her their private sign of approval.

"Thanks. I needed that," Sylvia quipped. "Now enough about gossip, it's time for business." And the day began, belatedly, to proceed normally.

By the end of that difficult Monday, Sylvia was feeling the makings of a super headache. All day she had either fenced with rude questions or ignored speculative looks until she was ready to scream at the next person who dared speak to her. She drove home in her new car, which also had been a source of questions, eager to enter her empty house and be alone in total peace and silence.

As she jumped out to raise the garage door, she remembered her date, and banged her head against the door simultaneously. She groaned aloud. Why had she agreed to go out with pretty Roy? She didn't know him, didn't have the same good feeling about him that she had for Craig, and still hadn't asked Aunt Willy about his father's family. And she didn't want to go anywhere tonight with anyone.

Her shoulders gave an unaccustomed sag as she returned to the car to drive into the garage. As she opened the door, she heard the clanking and grinding of Jody's old truck in the drive behind her. If he says one word about Craig, I'll punch him right in the nose, Sylvia promised herself, her violent thoughts about her favorite sibling surprising her.

"Good news, Sylvia!" Jody slammed the door of his truck shut and loped up the blacktop to where she stood waiting beside her Thunderbird. "I have a job interview. It pays double what I'm making now, and Carol can live in the city like she wants."

"Oh, Jody." All her irritation melted away in the face of his eager enthusiasm. "How wonderful. Where is it?"

"That's the only problem. It's in Massachusetts and I don't think my truck will make it that far. Can I borrow your car for a couple of days? Sylvia? Say something!"

The glazed expression on her face faded and she shook her head, hard, as if to clear it, her voice rising a little on each word. "My new car. My brand-new car. You want to borrow my car for *two days*, take it off to another state, and leave me *that* thing to drive!"

"Shhhhh. You'll hurt Bertha's feelings."

"That hunk of junk doesn't have enough parts to have feelings!"

"Oh, Sylvia." Jody placed his hands on her shoulders and gave her his best pleading look. "This is my big break. I've almost got the job, but I have to show for that interview."

How could she resist her carbon copy? With a deep sigh, Sylvia handed him the car keys. "I'll probably regret this two minutes after you drive away, so you'd better make it fast."

She was subjected to a violent hug and a big smacking kiss. "Thank's loads, Sylvia. You're the best sister a man could ever have."

"Sure," she muttered, "and I'm also out of my mind."

As she moved to let him slide into the driver's seat, the forlorn look on her face prompted Jody to speak. "Don't worry, Sylvia. I promise I won't wreck it."

Her eyes widened. "You'd better not, little brother. I'm just thinking of driving that miserable heap around."

Jody laughed. With the too-old lines smoothed from his face, he looked like her little brother again. "It's not so bad. If you have any trouble while I'm gone, Dad can fix it."

As he backed down the drive, Sylvia remembered the picture in the trunk. "Jody," she called. "Be sure to stop by Aunt Willy's house and take that picture in the trunk out of the car and leave it with her. It's for Momma's birthday. I'll have to wrap it while you're gone."

He nodded in agreement, turned the car smoothly into the street and cruised away with her lovely birthday present to herself.

"Mad. I'm utterly mad. The closer I get to thirty, the more my brain deteriorates," Sylvia muttered to herself as she entered the side door to her spacious kitchen.

Instead of the usual feeling of peace and contentment that cradled her when she walked into the house, a vague jarring note struck her. She hesitated briefly in the act of placing her briefcase on the table, then rested her hands lightly at her sides and slowly turned around to observe the entire room. What was it that caused that discordant note? There was no one else there—she could sense that the house was empty. And everything was in its place. But no, not quite.

There was no dust. Sylvia knew precisely how much dust leaked into the huge old house from the winds whipping the dirt from the streets and the minute amounts of soot that collected when the wood fire burned. The kitchen counters, the buffet, the corner china cabinets with her grandma's fine collection—all were polished clean and it had been two days since she'd had a chance to dust.

The uneasy feeling grew in Sylvia. Why would anyone bother to enter her house and dust? *Maybe they didn't want fingerprints to show.* Had anything been stolen?

She made a full pivot standing in the middle of the kitchen floor. China all there. She took a few steps and opened the buffet drawers. Grandma's silver all there. Her jewelry? She turned to use the back stairs. As she passed the cookie jar resting beside the flour canister, Sylvia stopped. She always kept the jar resting in the middle of the hairline crack in the old tiles to cover it. It had been moved, only a fraction of an inch. Nobody else would have noticed but Sylvia. She began to notice other subtle clues that spoke to her of someone messing with her things.

A fierce possessive anger built in Sylvia as she trod up the rear stairs and through the hidden door. She glanced through the upstairs rooms. Whoever had been there was good; Sylvia gave them their due. If the house hadn't been so completely hers, if she didn't have a fetish about keeping everything in its place, she would never have noticed that everything had been gone over.

In her bedroom, she went straight for her jewelry chest. Opening it, she found her diamonds winking back at her. And her pearls lay quietly waiting. Nothing was missing. Nothing. Underneath her anger seeped puzzlement. Who on earth would rummage through her house? And why?

Chapter Four

The clear ringing of the doorbell broke into Sylvia's thoughts. She gently lifted the curtain aside on her bedroom window and looked down at the tall male figure standing before her door. A tight, intense feeling gathered in her chest then faded as she realized it was not Craig, but Roy. She sighed as she visualized a boring evening discussing ancient relatives.

As Sylvia attempted to open the window, the swollen sash stuck, then slid up as she shoved it hard. Muttering words she was glad her students couldn't hear, she poked her head out the window and called down to the man on her step. "It's not locked. Come on in, Roy. I'll be right down."

She peeled off the formal pantsuit she had worn to school and replaced it with comfortable jeans and a pale lavender blouse, exchanged her heels for loafers and ran a comb through her hair. She was ready.

Stepping briskly down the formal front stairs, Sylvia noted that Roy was standing just inside the big double doors, staring into the living room. He seemed to be assessing the monetary value of each item within his sight. Her steps slowed as she watched his darting eyes. With that expression on his face, he didn't have his beautiful good looks. A strange chill rippled down her spine. He is not a nice man, she thought, then chastised herself. Next you'll be seeing dollar signs on his eyeballs. Don't let your imagination run wild, Sylvia, she scolded.

As he caught sight of Sylvia coming down the stairs, a perfect smile made his face perfectly pretty again. "Dad always said there were some fancy old houses in Devon. Guess this is one of them." The glib words rolled off his tongue and his eyes had an overeager gleam in them as he surveyed Sylvia's well-proportioned figure.

"Have you decided to take a survey of the contents of Devon houses?" Sylvia smiled politely at him to take the edge from her sharp query.

He gave her a startled look then broke into a raucous laugh as he stepped toward her. "You're a real joker." He laughed again and reached for her hand.

"Yeah," muttered Sylvia to herself as she disengaged his cold fingers. "I'm a laugh a minute." All she wanted to do was to get this evening over with so she could get back to her house early—alone. Fending off Roy's hands wasn't her idea of a fun evening. "Shall we go, Roy? I'm all ready for a pizza."

While they drove across town to John's Pizza, Roy made constant comments about the wealth, or lack of it, of the residents of the houses they passed. His emphasis on money began to irritate Sylvia.

"How can you make such blanket statements about people you don't know just from the looks of their houses?" Sylvia frowned at him. She didn't know why, but all this money talk was making her uneasy and so was the way Roy kept looking at her. Like she was another thing to be priced.

Flashing her his perfect smile, which was looking less perfect to Sylvia every minute, Roy told her, "It's easy. Some big ones aren't painted and need to be. And little things—like decorative trim, swimming pools, new screens—say that they have extra money to spend. New cars. Lots of signs, if you know how to look for them."

And you do, Sylvia thought. Now why is that? A sigh of relief eased out of her when they parked in the shopping center in front of the pizza place. Glancing at her watch, she promised herself that in two hours, at the most, she would be back home.

Ignoring the startled reaction behind the counter, Sylvia walked to a booth and seated herself, waiting for Roy to finish ordering and join her. *Yes, John. Two men in three days. How's that grab you?* Strange. She received no pleasure from the amazed looks sent her way. Being with Roy wasn't at all like being with Craig. Never again, she told herself. Never again will I accept a date just to have a date.

She rested her chin on her cupped hand, leaning on her elbow, and half listened to Roy as he seated himself and began to chatter. Your basic nonsense, she thought, hoping she wouldn't embarrass herself by falling asleep.

A shadow loomed over her shoulder and inexplicably her heart began to beat faster. She was not at all surprised when a large hand grasped her shoulder firmly and a deep voice rumbled above her.

"Fancy meeting you here, Sylvia. Who's your friend?" After Sylvia made a brief introduction, Craig continued, "Mind if I join you?"

Without waiting for an answer, he pushed his bulk into the booth, forcing Sylvia to slide over or be crushed. Even though she was smack against the wall, she was unable to escape touching him. The shifting movements he made to get his large body comfortable in the small booth caused his leg to rub against hers, the pressure increasing, then relaxing. Sylvia pressed her fingers together, trying to ignore the churning feeling in her stomach. It's just crowded, woman, calm down, she cautioned herself. You're not eighteen anymore.

John marched over and slid two pizzas onto the table in front of them.

Craig offered an explanation in response to the puzzled looks on the faces of his companions. "I phoned in mine."

A petulant look crossed Roy's face, marring his beauty again. Sylvia couldn't help comparing the faces of the two men. Roy's perfectly formed features lacked the character that Craig's rough countenance had. The strength in Craig went deeper than the sheer physical power he obviously possessed. Roy was a butterfly flitting here and there, trying to find the most nectar, Sylvia thought, while Craig was a rock mountain, steady and dependable. And sexy, she added as his knee rubbed against hers.

Roy frowned at Craig. "You have a lot of nerve. Sylvia is my date."

"Oh, I don't think so." Craig spoke very softly. "Friend—maybe. Dinner companion—definitely. But date—no. No, I don't think so at all."

A red flush crept up Roy's neck and colored his fair complexion. "Just who do you think you are?"

"Sylvia's lover." Craig smiled blandly as Sylvia gasped and Roy turned purple.

"Craig, you liar," Sylvia whispered to him, pushing away the brief wish that it were true.

Encouraged by her outraged face, Roy threatened Craig. "You're annoying the lady. If you don't leave, I'll throw you out."

Craig snorted. "You and who else? But I will leave—as long as you understand one thing."

Are they going to fight? Oh, I hope not. Sylvia reached for the pizza and took a big bite to calm her nerves.

As Craig pushed himself out of the seat, his hand fell on Sylvia's thigh and the gentle caress that followed caused her to choke on the mouthful of pizza she was trying to chew. She cut her eyes sideways at him, not daring to turn her head. He was smiling! The beast.

"Want me to do the Heimlich maneuver?" the beast bent and whispered in her ear.

"No I do not." The words came out thick and hoarse. All due to the choking spell, of course.

Roy's cold, flat voice broke into her confused thoughts. "Just what am I supposed to understand?"

Craig straightened. Looking down at Roy, he spoke calmly, but with a firm strength. "The lady belongs to me. Don't tamper with her."

"Craig!" She should be insulted at his presumption. Highly insulted. Then why was she so relieved that Roy would think she had a protector?

Roy's eyes narrowed and his nostrils enlarged as he took in the penetrating look Craig gave Sylvia and the way she avoided his eyes. "Are you threatening me?"

Sylvia was reminded of the hiss of a snake and she shivered in the warm booth. Her eyes were drawn to the tension on the two faces and she was appalled by the visible hate etched on Roy's.

Craig was unmoved by the fierceness of Roy's reply. He stood with his arms folded, his bulk towering above the booth. "Only if Sylvia gets hurt," he replied.

Why did she get the impression that these two men meant far more with their words than what they said? What was going on here as each fought for mastery with only his eyes?

When he was satisfied that Roy understood him, Craig picked up his box of pizza and turned to go. "I'll see you later, Sylvia," he tossed out, then left.

Strained silence stretched between Roy and Sylvia. She nervously swallowed another bite of pizza without tasting it at all. What a waste of good food, she thought, then glanced over at the scowl on Roy's face and supposed she should say something—anything. Maybe apologize for Craig's behavior.

"Why didn't you tell me about him?"

The venom in Roy's voice startled Sylvia and she dropped the piece of pizza into her lap. It slid upside down across her jeans and onto the floor under the table. "Good grief," she muttered, grabbing a napkin and dabbing at the tomato stains on her denims. "Tell you what?" she answered sharply. "That he lives? That I've met him?" She threw the soiled napkin onto the table. "I certainly didn't know he was going to be here tonight."

"You didn't act like you minded much."

"What of it?" The nerve of the twerp!

Roy edged forward and smiled. It was not a pretty smile. "You'll be sorry if you cooperate with him and not with us."

That did it. Sylvia shoved the pizza back and slid out of the booth. "I don't know what you're talking about and I don't really care. I'm going home. No, don't bother to get up. I'll walk."

A snicker edged Roy's voice. "You won't walk all the way home."

"Watch me."

Sylvia turned her back and marched out of the pizza joint. Just as she pushed open the door, she caught a glimpse of John's open mouth and a giggle almost bubbled up to spoil her foul mood. John was having a little trouble coping with the fact that she was actually walking out on a date.

Once outside, Sylvia took a couple of deep breaths, then she looked back in the window at Roy. He was leaning back leisurely, as if waiting for her to come back in and ask him to please drive her home. Fat chance.

Long strides carried her swiftly down the edge of the highway back to town, where she cut across a few backyards and a vacant lot to take a shortcut home. Her anger fueled her feet and she slowed her pace only to remove a pebble from her shoe, then strode ahead. What a drip Roy had turned out to be. *From now on, Sylvia, always trust your instincts.*

Ah, the last block just ahead. She turned the corner, her comfortable shoes making slight thudding sounds as she slowed her pace. The strange tension that she'd felt in Roy's presence had faded as she'd walked home, but now, as she approached her house, the vague uneasiness returned. The angry roar of a motor ripped apart the quiet air and a car zipped around the corner and jerked to a halt beside her.

"Broads don't walk out on me." Roy snarled at her through the open window. "Get in."

"I must decline your so-kind invitation." Sylvia smiled at him though her green eyes glittered in a manner Jody would have recognized. "As you can see my abode is just ahead and I am no longer in need of your chariot."

Muttering words Sylvia rarely heard and didn't even know she knew, Roy threw the car door open and jumped out. "We have things to talk about. Now!" He reached out and yanked Sylvia's arm.

"Mistake number three." Sylvia spit the words at him as she doubled her other fist and slammed it into Roy's nose.

He screamed and clutched his hands to his face. Sylvia noted with deep satisfaction that blood was seeping through his fingers before she turned and ran up the walk to her front door. Jody would have been proud of her. That was a punch he had taught her. Sliding quickly through the door, Sylvia locked it behind her and flicked off her porch light.

Vulgar words spewed from Roy's mouth and fouled the clean evening air as he stomped up her sidewalk in the dark. Sylvia could imagine the shocked responses of her neighbors, who would be listening avidly. She leaned against the door and waited for him, ignoring her shaking fingers. Abruptly the profanity stopped. A curious scuffling sound followed by thuds and a groan penetrated Sylvia's solid door. Then silence.

What on earth was going on?

Three loud knocks in rapid succession echoed in the foyer, causing Sylvia to jump nervously away from the door. Again the knocking came. The nerve of that man, Sylvia thought. Maybe he wants another punch. Looking around for a weapon, she caught up an umbrella from the hall stand. As she yanked open the door, she thrust the point of the umbrella into the darkness and felt it collide with a solid object.

A loud grunt. "Damnation!" Bushes crashed with the weight of a heavy body. "Sylvia, will you put that thing away," a familiar deep voice rumbled.

"Craig? Is that you?"

"What's left of me." Branches crackled.

Sylvia flicked on the light and stared at the remains of her lilacs nestled around Craig's solid form. She carefully kept from smiling at the disgruntled look on his face. "What are you doing smashing my shrubs?" Without waiting for a reply, she glanced about the yard nervously. "Where's Roy?"

"Number one: I got here trying to escape that stupid thing you're holding which connected with my ribs. Number two: pretty Roy, who at the moment is no longer pretty, has been persuaded to leave."

Sylvia stopped gazing around the yard and concentrated on Craig's face. His shirt was torn and a large bruise graced his cheek. Long scratches ran down his arms and one hand was held tightly to his ribs.

"Oh, Craig. Did he hurt you?" She rushed forward to help him out of the bushes.

Craig's crooked grin wobbled at her as he hoisted himself up. "Not half as much as your umbrella and lilacs."

She draped his arm around her shoulder and guided him inside the door, kicking it shut behind them. "What are you doing here, anyway?"

Tucking his own arm around Sylvia, Craig headed straight for the living room, taking her with him. He eased himself down onto the couch and looked up at her, the corners of his mouth twitching. "Would you believe protecting you? I was waiting behind the bushes to make sure that goon didn't molest you when you came home."

How sweet. It had been years since anyone had thought of protecting her. "Then I stabbed you with my umbrella and knocked you into my lilacs. Poor dear."

Sylvia made a sympathizing sound and knelt before Craig, reaching for the buttons of his shirt. In a few deft movements she had it opened to his waist and was examining the ugly gash on his chest and the multicolored area surrounding it while valiantly ignoring the expanse of naked flesh.

Craig winced as her fingers delicately probed the ribs underneath the damaged flesh.

"Nothing broken. Stay right here."

He watched her swaying hips as she moved swiftly through the swinging doors into the kitchen. *Nice.* He felt a tightening response in his groin and grinned. *Not to worry, Sylvia. I'm not going anywhere.* Stretching his long legs out, he leaned down and made himself comfortable against the large cushions on the couch as he listened to banging cupboards and slamming drawers.

Soon Sylvia returned with a jumble of objects cradled in her arms. She stopped in the doorway to look at him lying on her couch, and a feeling that could only be attributed to her anxious hormones washed over her at the sight of his naked chest cuddled among her sofa pillows. Good grief. And she had thought she was going to treat his wound just as casually as she used to fix Jody's.

Taking a deep breath, Sylvia spoke brightly. "Dr. Sylvia to the rescue."

The complacent look fled Craig's face at the sight of all the bandages and sharp objects in her arms. "What are you planning to do? Dress wounds for an army?" He half rose and crossed his hands protectively in front of his chest. "Can't you put that stuff away and just give me a big kiss of thanks?"

"That is precisely what I am not going to do," Sylvia muttered and clamped her lips together. "Lie down and be still." The stuff she carried in her arms tumbled to the floor as she knelt down beside the couch and pushed him backwards.

Gritting his teeth, Craig submitted to the iodine wash and watched as she laid out bandages, scissors and tape. When she picked up a square green metal box and opened it to reveal a thick yellow salve inside, he asked suspiciously, "What's that?"

"Bag balm."

"It has a picture of a cow on it."

"So it does." She dug a finger into the salve and reached to rub it on his wound.

Grabbing her hand, he held her finger away from him. "I am not a cow." Picking up the metal box, he read the small print on the label. "Sylvia..." His voice rumbled deeper than usual. "I do not have an udder."

Sylvia laughed at the glowering look he gave her. "I know that, silly." She yanked her hand away and quickly smeared the medicine on his gash, popped the bandage on and taped it over the area. Then she leaned back on her heels and smirked at him.

"If I turn into a cow, I will..."

She collapsed forward onto his chest, giggling helplessly. "Bag balm was Grandma's favorite remedy for whatever we kids did to ourselves when we visited her." She raised her head with the laughter still in her eyes and caught the intense look on his face.

As Craig slid his hand up her back and gathered a handful of her thick hair into his fist, her laughter fled. Tiny slivers of sheer passion splintered and expanded to an exploding intensity. The depths of her green eyes glittered with an emotion far different from anger. His large hand twined in her hair and guided her head closer, closer, until his mouth tasted hers.

Her hands wouldn't stay in her lap, like nice girls' hands. Instead they crept to Craig's opened shirt and began to explore his chest. Edging around the bandage, she found and traced the smooth flesh that covered his tight muscles.

Craig felt her light touches multiply and divide, tracing unseen paths that left no trail, except the multiplying sensations she was producing in him, causing him to deepen his kiss and pull her closer to him.

Sylvia was drowning in the delicious swirls of passion that circled and returned, ever increasing, ever building. She felt Craig's strong fingers moving through her hair and knew that she had to stop it soon, but she didn't want to; she wanted to continue kissing him, wanted— What did she want? *Sylvia, get a hold on yourself. The man's only going to be here one week.*

Reluctantly, she pulled away. "No, Craig." Pushing his hand away from her she tilted back on her toes, her green eyes wide as she watched him. "You've got to go."

Craig lay back, lacing his hands behind his head to hide the faint tremors that shot through his body, interfering with his steady control. He cocked his head to one side at her. "If I move, I might get gangrene."

"I doubt it."

"I haven't had any of that popcorn you bought for me yet."

"Out, Craig."

"There's a good movie on TV tonight."

"Craig, I don't want you to make love to me. If you stay here . . . I . . . I don't trust what might happen."

"Sylvia." Craig sat up and swung his legs to the floor. "I promise I'll never do anything you don't want me to do."

"*That* is precisely what I'm afraid of: what I want you to do," Sylvia explained. She bent to pick up her nursing equipment and missed the flash in his dark eyes at her confession. "I might want you to make love to me on a primitive level, but I don't want to have a real affair," she continued as she scooped the stuff into her arms.

"What if I solemnly promise that I will not try to seduce you, not once tonight? Will you let me stay? Please? I'm hungry."

"Not once?"

"Solemn promise."

More's the pity, one part of Sylvia thought, and she was immediately scandalized by her mind's wanderings. She battered down those uncomfortable urges and smiled faintly at Craig. "I'm hungry too. Because of you, I didn't get to eat my pizza."

A wickedly satisfied look crossed Craig's face. "Did a good job of making him mad, didn't I?"

Recalling the hatred in Roy's eyes, Sylvia slowly nodded. "He was too mad." She frowned and hugged her armful of stuff while she remembered. "And he said some strange things."

Craig's indolent air fled and he quickly pushed up on one elbow to stare intently at Sylvia. "What things?"

How could she tell Craig those silly things? Roy had been a real jerk. Anyway, he was gone from both their lives, just a man passing through. Then she recalled that Craig was also a man just passing through and a shadow darkened her face. She shrugged. "It wasn't important." Jumping up, she headed for the kitchen. "I'll get rid of this stuff."

Now what was that all about? Craig frowned after her. Why hadn't she wanted to talk about Roy Pratty? And why the dark look on her face? Heaving himself all the way up from her couch caused his bruises to introduce themselves and Craig winced as he stood up and smiled grimly at himself. Getting to be a namby-pamby, Craig? he asked himself as he let his shirt fall to the floor. Letting a few bushes get the best of you? Letting a good-looking woman go to your head? Just remember why you're here.

"How do you want your popcorn?" Sylvia's voice floated in from the kitchen, interrupting his silent monologue.

"Is there more than one way?" A few long strides and Craig was in the kitchen with her, with his crooked grin.

Sylvia drew a quick breath at the sight of his gorgeous chest with all those bare muscles, then stirred her faltering self-control by telling herself that she absolutely refused to fall for his overgrown boyish charm. Popcorn and TV. That was all. "Of course." She looked from one popcorn popper on the counter to another. "Hot air or grease. Then there's butter, cheese, garlic powder or—"

He was moving closer, hovering over her. Not touching her. Oh, no. Just being there, his hearty masculine presence reaching out to her. Sylvia gritted her teeth.

"I like greasy, salty, cheesy popcorn." His breath was warm on her forehead and she could see the gentle movements of the smooth flesh on his chest. "And I like to lick . . . my fingers afterward."

Good grief. What sexy images his deep rumbling words conjured up. And he probably intended her to see every fantasy that flickered behind her eyelids. He wasn't playing fair. Then a delightful idea popped into her fertile brain and she smiled wickedly at Craig.

Reaching out, she seized his rough hand and brought it to her mouth. Carefully running her tongue around each finger, she slowly moistened and licked, while keeping her eyes on his. "Like this?" she asked in a low voice, and had the satisfaction of seeing his pupils dilate and the midnight blackness grow even denser.

"You're a wicked woman, Sylvia Perkins," Craig rasped at her.

"Serves you right." She dropped his hand and moved away to fix the popcorn, mischievous lights in her eyes dancing. "You be good, and I will, too."

"You mean all we get is popcorn and TV?"

Sylvia wanted to laugh at the mournful look on his face, but decided it might not be wise at the moment. "You've got it."

"Okay, you win." Craig spoke in such a cheerful voice that Sylvia glanced at him suspiciously. "But next time is *my* night."

"Who said there'd be a next time?" Sylvia turned and glared at him, angry with herself for wanting a next time. "You shouldn't even be here. This pretend affair is supposed to be for the benefit of my family and they don't even know you're here. Maybe you should leave now."

The ring of her telephone cut through the chill left by her hostile words and she yanked the receiver off the wall.

"Hello." She straightened and her face lit up. "How do you know there's a man in my house, Aunt Willy?" A broad grin spread over Sylvia's face and her eyes sparkled at Craig. "Ah, yes. Mrs. Winegath across the street. No, he's not leaving soon. In fact he may stay the night." She held the phone away from her ear to escape the loud squawking noises and spoke quickly. "Got to go, Aunt Willy. Give my love to all. Bye-Bye."

Craig suppressed a smile as they exchanged amused glances. "Does this mean I get to stay?"

"Durn tootin'." Sylvia's stubborn chin was tilted upward. "We'll watch movies all night long."

Craig laughed softly and drew Sylvia to him with his long, muscular arms. "I must remember to thank Aunt Willy someday," he said as his lips grazed the tip of her nose, then landed safely in her hair. He gave her a hard squeeze and released her so suddenly that she almost lost her balance. "Don't burn the popcorn."

"So—now you prefer the popcorn to the person. My feelings are hurt," she chattered on as she pulled out a bowl and dumped the contents of the popper into it, salting it before she glanced up at him. He stood motionless and the burning light in his eyes caused her words to catch in her throat and fade away. "Craig—don't."

His answer was husky and seemed to come from far away. "No law against lookin', lady." Then he seized the bowl of popcorn and led the way back into the living room.

By mutual consent they kept the conversation light after that. During the second movie, with the popcorn long gone, Sylvia began to get sleepy and she yawned so wide that Craig laughed at her and offered her his lap for her head.

"Tempting offer, but I'm getting chilly. Let me run up and get a couple of quilts and pillows. We can lie on the floor."

Craig nodded his approval and Sylvia hastily climbed the front stairs and rummaged in her linen closet to find the items. Calling to Craig, she tossed the heavy patchwork quilts down the stairs. They tumbled and flipped down the treads and slipped to a stop at his feet. He picked them up and waited for her to descend with a pillow clutched under each arm.

They made themselves comfortable on the floor in front of the television, lying separately on the pillows, stomachs down, heads propped on elbows, each covered with a separate quilt. But Sylvia could sense the entire length of Craig stretched out beside her. This was a really dumb idea, Sylvia, she told herself. At least before we were sitting up.

The movie was an arty love story. Sylvia thought that the hero was a boring wimp and the heroine deserved more. Too bad she can't have my hero, she caught herself thinking and was a little scared at the thought. *Watch it, ole girl. Craig is not yours in any shape or form.*

Depression lowered her head to the pillow and she ignored the flickering screen, closing her eyes to shut out niggling truths that wanted to be heard. The sounds of the TV receded and faded as Sylvia succumbed to the easy temptation the pillow offered her and slept.

After his comments on the show had gone repeatedly unanswered, Craig nudged Sylvia and spoke her name. She lay unmoving, with her breathing coming deep and slow. He smiled and moved his pillow next to hers, turning and drawing her warmth against him. His last thought before drifting off to join her was how right she felt against him.

Chapter Five

Noise. Pounding. Pounding. Sylvia rubbed her eyes and raised her head from the pillow. The TV set still had people moving across the screen in their fantasy world of tragedy. Was that what had awakened her?

A heavy weight rested across her legs, hindering movement, and she turned her head to find Craig snuggled against her, fast asleep, with one leg thrown over hers. She rolled her head away from him, so she wouldn't have to look at the broad lines of his face nestled close to her and want to reach out and touch him.

Again came the demanding, insistent noise. Someone was knocking on her door. Wondering why they didn't just ring the bell, Sylvia struggled to slide out from under Craig's leg, and his eyes flickered and sprang open.

"What's wrong?"

"Someone's knocking at the door."

Craig glanced at his watch. "At 2:00 a.m.?" He was instantly alert and rolled to his feet. "I'll take care of it."

"You most certainly will not. This is my house and I'll take care of it," Sylvia replied, cutting in front of him as he moved toward the front door.

They reached the door at the same moment and Sylvia switched on the outside light while Craig opened the door. The uniformed officer standing on the front steps blinked under the sudden bright light.

"Sylvia Perkins?"

"Yes."

"Do you own a new Thunderbird?"

Oh, God. Something's happened to Jody. "Yes. What's the matter, Officer?"

The young trooper turned and gestured at the parked state patrol car behind him and another officer opened the door and stood up. A third man slid out and leaned on him. They walked up the sidewalk together.

"Is this your brother, ma'am?"

Jody. He was all right, thank God. She started to answer, "Yes, he's my brother," but all she could do was stare in horror at him as he staggered up to her door supported by the shoulder of the other trooper.

Swollen black eyes dominated his face. His lower lip was cut and had been bleeding. His only suit was ripped and muddied, totally ruined. One arm curled possessively around his abdomen as he stopped on the bottom step and stared up at Sylvia, the look in his eyes reminding her of the day almost twenty years before when he'd been the one to tell her about her dead puppy.

"Sylvia . . . I couldn't . . . stop them."

She reached out and took his arm. "Get in here and sit down before you fall down."

"If you don't mind, we'll be going now."

Her attention refocused on the freckles and light hair of the officer and her eyes narrowed. "Is that you, Sandy Daniels? You get in here too—both of you," she ordered. "Just what is the meaning of bringing my brother here like this?"

Both officers entered the door at the same time, offering soothing words, but Sylvia refused to listen to them until they were all in the living room and Jody was seated on the couch, sinking back gratefully into the softness of the upholstery. The patrolmen seated themselves uneasily on either side of him.

She barely heard Craig's offer to make coffee and nodded in agreement before turning to the three men. "Now, I want an explanation and it had better be good." She looked at Jody, but his face was in his hands. "Well?" She looked questioningly at the officer with whom she had once gone to school and her temper began to simmer on slow boil.

"We had nothing to do with Jody's condition—honest, Sylvia. This is the way we picked him up, and after listening to his story, we brought him to you, as he asked."

"Then why did you act like I was a stranger?"

A bright flush graced the young man's cheeks. "I didn't know if you'd remember me."

Sylvia threw up her hands at such male logic and turned back to her brother. "Jody?" Sylvia went to him and knelt on the floor before him, lifting his head to force him to look at her. "What happened, Jody? Please tell me."

"I tried, but I couldn't." Tears shimmered in his eyes. "There were two of them."

Jody crying? Jody never cried no matter how badly he was hurt. Jody only cried when someone else mattered.

"What couldn't you do?" She asked the question gently, taking the cup of coffee Craig silently handed her and tucking it into Jody's hands. A brief smile of thanks to Craig and a warm thought of how nice it was to have him here flitted through her mind, then she returned her attention to Jody.

"I couldn't stop them."

"Jody, will you just tell me what happened!" She covered his cold fingers with her hands.

His eyes looked ancient as he began to recite his story. "I left later than I'd planned, stopping at Aunt Willy's, picking up some diapers at the store and taking them back home, so it was almost seven when I got on the road—I was going to get on the turnpike at Waterville." He took several gulps of the strong coffee and continued.

"I was almost to the turnoff, when this pickup truck came whizzing past—I never saw a pickup go that fast—then it stopped down the road a ways, and these two guys got out and just stood in the road. I had to stop to keep from hitting them. One was in his fifties, with this weird hat pulled down with just his beady eyes sticking out under it and the other was early thirties, blond, good lookin'—he did all the talkin'. I thought they had engine trouble."

He grimaced, then winced at the pain in his split lip. "Instead, I was the one that had trouble."

"Jody, pleeeease. Get to the point."

"They beat me up and..." The words trailed off. "Took your car."

"They did what?" Sylvia rocked back on her heels and made a valiant effort to control her rising temper. "Repeat that, please."

He covered his face again. "They stole your car." The words were said with such emptiness that Sylvia was alarmed.

"Jody, you don't think I'd blame you?"

"You don't?" A faint light shone in his eyes.

"Of course not. I'm just glad you're not hurt worse." She hugged him fiercely. "It's just a car, and you're my brother."

He smiled at her and his split lip cracked and a trickle of blood welled up in the crack.

"Oh, Jody. You have to go to the hospital."

"No. I'll be all right. I'll just go home."

"You certainly can't drive that rattletrap tonight."

Craig stepped forward. "My car is parked on the next block. I'll get it and be right back."

Sylvia gave him a grateful look and thanked Sandy and his fellow officer for bringing Jody to her. After she promised to file a stolen car report in the morning, the troopers left. Craig was out the door also before Sylvia noticed the extra coffee cups. He must have given them coffee, too. She felt a rush of warmth. He'd been there, helping, when she'd needed him, no questions, no taking over, just helping.

A wistful little smile played around her mouth and her eyes softened as she gazed at the two pillows and quilts crumpled on the floor. The TV was silent. Craig must have turned it off while she had been listening to Jody.

Jody followed the direction of her misty eyes and took in the indented pillows and bedding tossed aside. "Were you sleeping with him?" His tone was hostile, demanding.

"As a matter of fact, I was." Her chin was up, and her tone was equally hostile. It was no lie. She had been sleeping soundly.

"Sylvia." Jody reached out to take her hand, his voice gentled. "I don't want to see you hurt."

"Then don't you start on me, too."

"I won't. But we don't know anything about this guy. Maybe he hired those thugs to steal your car. One said something funny to me, something about my sister's cooperation."

"Don't be an idiot. How could they know me? And why would Craig do a thing like that?"

"I don't know. Maybe he wants you where he can keep an eye on you."

"That's one of the silliest things you've ever said and I'm going to pretend that you never did." But she couldn't. Was there any truth to Jody's suppositions? But why would Craig do it? Then she thought of how those beastly men had attacked Jody and taken her new car. *They took my car. My new car. My birthday present to myself—and I hadn't even changed tags yet.* For some reason that last fact was important to her.

When Craig returned, she was subdued and avoided his eyes. What if Jody were right? Was Craig really a threat to them? She sure hadn't felt threatened last night. She sighed, a slow drawn out breath, and thrust aside her own doubts to help Jody to Craig's car. After he lay down in the back seat, Sylvia walked to Jody's old truck and started the motor. Backing out the truck, she drove slowly across town, so Craig could follow her.

After they had gotten Jody home, explained to Carol what had happened and calmed her down, the early light of morning was beginning to streak the eastern sky. Finally they were able to leave and return to Sylvia's house. Too many confused thoughts went back and forth, back and forth in her tired mind, and she didn't feel like talking about any of them, especially to Craig, not after the suspicion Jody had placed in her mind.

At her door, Sylvia pushed her hair behind her ears in a tired gesture and turned to Craig. "Just go, Craig, please. I need to be alone and I have to be at school in a couple of hours."

He gave her a searching look. "What happened to that friendly rapport we had? I feel a distinct chill radiating from you."

"Not now, Craig."

His steady black eyes looked at her. "Okay, Sylvia, but tonight I'll be back, and we'll talk."

The grim determination in his raspy voice told Sylvia that he would indeed expect an explanation of her behavior, and she wasn't sure that she could give one. Wasn't even sure that she wanted to. Averting her eyes, she avoided replying to his statement and ducked into her house, shutting him on the outside.

Now what is going on? Craig stared at the closed door, his huge fists shoved into the wide pockets of his pants. Was she blackmailing the Prattys? Was that why they took her car and beat up her brother? That's who it had to be, with that description fitting both Roy and Freddy, but where was Jerry? Holed up somewhere? Then how were they going to get the information coordinated? Was Sylvia their go-between? And why was she suddenly avoiding him?

So many questions. Craig drove off in his car to the nearest pay telephone, hoping to find a few answers about Sylvia, knowing that the answers to some equally important questions about her could only be answered by himself, and also knowing that he was unwilling even to ask those questions.

At that moment Sylvia was feeling equally unwilling to ask probing questions of herself about Craig, and was climbing her stairs to tumble onto the bed for an hour before facing her students—unprepared, and with their papers ungraded for the second time this week.

When her alarm clock buzzed a short time later she contemplated throwing it across the room, but decided, no—she'd paid too much for the stupid thing to ruin it. Pushing in the switch, she silenced the noise and rolled off the bed. A shower, a little on the cool side, helped her wake up.

Dressing in a deep peach suit with an oyster-white blouse, because she knew she would need to look well, since she felt so horrible, Sylvia cocked her head and smiled at herself in the mirror. Big gold hoops, a gift from her mother that she'd never worn, hung from her ears. Yes, these earrings were definitely suitable for a woman having an affair.

Then her smile dimmed and she remembered that she had tried to forget that her "affairee" might have been responsible for her brother's beating. Could she have judged wrongly this time?

"Oh, no," Sylvia said aloud, and could have groaned as she remembered she had no way to get to school. She couldn't call Jody. He needed rest. She'd call her sister, Betty. She'd be up, anyway, to get Sara off to kindergarten.

After she'd called and explained why she needed a ride, Sylvia knew it was only a matter of hours before the entire family would descend on Jody and Carol, carrying food and bearing unwanted advice, so she made a quick call to Carol to warn her. Betty drove up while she was still on the phone so she hurriedly said her goodbyes, grabbed her briefcase, and slipped out the door.

Her sister glanced at her own tousled blond head and frayed sweatshirt in the rearview mirror and looked back at Sylvia's suit and smoothly turned pageboy. "You're disgusting. Looking like that this early."

Sylvia knew her baby sister, who was only twenty-two, could look like a model when she wanted to and only grinned at her. "You're still as grouchy as ever in the mornings, I see. Pregnant again?"

"No! And don't let Bob hear you say that. He wants another one."

"Two isn't enough?"

"He wants four!"

"Let him stay home and take care of them while you go to work."

Betty turned the last street corner before Devon High and pulled to a stop in front of the school, then she turned to answer Sylvia. "I think you're nuts, Sylvia. But it's worth a try." She grinned at her older sister, a version of Sylvia's own devilish grin.

"There's hope for you yet, Sis." Sylvia hopped out. "Thanks for the ride."

"There's hope for you too," Betty replied, her grin widening as she peered out the window at Sylvia.

"What do you mean?"

"That Craig. Mmmm. Nice."

"Oh, Betty. For heaven's sake!" Sylvia stalked into the school without looking back, ignoring the delighted laughter floating from her sister's car as she drove off. She caught herself actually wishing there was hope for her with Craig. *Stop it, Sylvia.*

As she walked past the teachers' lounge to go straight to her room, an image swam before Sylvia's eyes of Craig, shirtless, muscles rippling, arms reaching out to enfold her. She stopped short, staring with a glazed expression at the lockers lining the wall and saw his mouth hovering, descending.

"Miz Perkins? Miz Perkins—you all right?"

The young worried voice penetrated Sylvia's fog and Jimmy Johnston's face materialized before her. "Why...yes, Jimmy. Thank you. I was just thinking." She smiled her teacher-smile and moved on down the corridor to her homeroom. What a liar you are, Sylvia, she told herself. You're not all right and you know it.

An uneasy feeling that things hadn't finished going wrong yet persisted and Sylvia was rewarded for her intuitive feelings by fidgety students who dangled their participles and confused adverbial and adjectival phrases. Then the cuff button from her blouse fell off, she couldn't find it, and her brand new hose ran like a race horse. Mr. Lord dropped by for one of his surprise evaluations amid the pandemonium of her level-four literature class acting out an improvised version of *Macbeth*. And that was just in the morning.

At noon break Sylvia was sure her premonition had been fulfilled and headed for the teachers' room for a much needed shot of caffeine, when the intercom blatted out her name. "Miss Perkins, telephone. Miss Perkins, telephone call in the office."

After she said her breathless hello into the phone and found out she was talking to Sandy Daniels, state trooper, she found her creeping unease unrelieved and growing stronger. His next words confirmed her suspicions.

"We think we know where your car is. We got an anonymous phone tip."

"Where?"

"In the old slate quarry at Colonial Junction."

"What! But that's filled with water!"

"That's the tip we got from our informant."

"Sandy, this isn't making any sense. Why would anyone steal my new car and then dump it? Wouldn't they try to sell it?"

"Maybe. Maybe not. Maybe it got too hot for them."

"Then why did they beat Jody up to get it?"

"I'm sure I don't know, Sylvia. We need you to come down after school to make a positive identification."

"A positive identification," Sylvia mimicked. "Sandy, you sound so official—or should I call you Officer Daniels?"

"Sylvia, we climbed trees together. You can call me anything."

Even though Sylvia wasn't feeling particularly happy, she laughed at Sandy. "I'll be there right after school," she promised him. After she hung up, she called Jody and told him, asking him if he felt like driving her over in his old truck. He insisted he was fine and would be at the school at three-thirty.

The rest of the day blurred for Sylvia. Conscious only of the passage of time, not of what she said to her classes, at one point she was surprised by the startled looks on her students as she discussed some of Shakespeare's favorite themes.

She stopped and asked, "What did I just say, Becky?"

The petite girl giggled. "You...you said that Shakespeare likes to steal cars and kisses good."

Good heavens! I'd better stop before I ruin a year's work, Sylvia thought, and told her class she was just testing to see if they were listening and that they would have the rest of the period for reading homework.

Using the homework technique in her next class also, she made it through to three o'clock. Then she carefully stacked papers to be graded into neat piles in her briefcase along with an extra red pen because the one she had at home was running out of ink. All the time she fiddled so precisely with her supplies, waiting for Jody, her mind was churning and fermenting ideas, possibilities, and why's.

At three-thirty-five, Jody's old truck clanked into the school driveway and rattled to a halt in the parking lot. Sylvia climbed in and rested her briefcase on the floor beside her feet.

Letting her gaze rest briefly on Jody as he pulled into the street, she frowned as she noted that while the swelling was subsiding on his face, the bruises were darker and bloodshot streaks marred his green eyes.

As he saw her mouth open, Jody hastily spoke. "I've been to Dr. Armstrong and my eyes will be fine, just colorful for several days."

"You're telling me the truth?"

"Would I lie to my big sister?"

The severe look Sylvia tried to keep in place kept slipping and a wispy grin slipped out. "You've tried before."

"You always knew even when you didn't rat on me."

"Oh, Jody." She could hold the words and feeling in no longer. "If anything worse had happened to you because of me, I'd just die."

"Hey, nutty sister. Something did happen to me, but it wasn't because of you."

"I'm not so sure. I have a feeling that..." Sylvia left her sentence unfinished, uncertain why she felt so strongly that Jody's beating had a purpose other than simple car theft. What had he said those men had talked about? Something about cooperation? Now why did that ring a bell? She curled her toes inside her shoes and pushed against the floor as she braced her briefcase against a curve.

Jody drove silently without arguing.

No one in Sylvia's family argued with her about her feelings because, more often than not, her feelings turned out to be an accurate barometer of what was going to happen.

Turning onto the rough road to the old slate quarry, Jody slowed his truck to a crawl, the worn shocks absorbing almost none of the bumps. Sylvia held tightly to the edge of the seat, trying to save her teeth, and for a brief moment let a wishful thought about her lovely, smooth-riding car flicker into the edges of her mind, then abruptly rejected it. What was done was done. One must be philosophical about it.

Or so she thought.

Two state police cars were parked near the quarry and a massive crane was resting beside the edge of the cliff. A third car came into view as Jody circled to the other side of the huge machine before parking the truck.

Well, well, Sylvia thought, as she wondered why Craig was there and how he knew where to be. What right did he have to stand there being buddy-buddy with her Maine State Troopers when he was just passing through? And what right did he have to be so darn sexy, she fumed as she closed the gap between them.

Jeans. Nobody had the right to look like that in jeans. Positively indecent. Sylvia looked at his powerful legs outlined in the faded denims and his knotted arm muscles as he gestured in the short-sleeved knit shirt while talking to Sandy Daniels. He had to know she was there—no one could miss the noise Jody's truck made. His hair was mussed as though he had been working, and Sylvia wanted to touch it, to wrap it around her fingers and lose her hands in the blackness of it, even as she could lose herself in the darkness of his eyes.

As though her spirit drew his, Craig turned to face her when she was directly behind him. A subtle thread was there weaving through the air, back and forth, between them, a gossamer piece of lightness woven of laughter, shared memories, and a hint, a promise, an echo of color and sound, drawing, binding them each to each. And only Craig and Sylvia saw, heard, felt the soothing chains. She could not move, could only look into Craig's rough countenance and wonder at the gentleness she saw reflected in his eyes.

But why is he here?

As though he sensed her faint withdrawal, Craig took a half step toward her. "Hello, Sylvia." Keeping his eyes fixed upon her, he acknowledged Jody also.

"Fancy meeting you here." Sylvia waited for an explanation from Craig, but he merely pulled her alongside him and casually turned back to Sandy and his partner. The view of the crane and worker was perfect from that angle and before Sylvia could begin to probe Craig to find out why he was there, the divers surfaced, climbed out on the ladder clamped to the cliff and signaled to the crane operator to take it up.

Tension splayed up Sylvia's spine and quivered. Would her car really come up out of that cold, watery pit? The heavy sound of the motor filled the air and resonated through her body. Thick cables cradled the automobile that was beginning to break through the jade-tinted water. Red. It was red.

The car swung up into the air. Sylvia's brand-new red Thunderbird hung from the crane like the victim of a huge spider dangling from its web. Hanging. Swaying. Dripping wet. And—

Sylvia didn't even hear the violent sentence that exploded from her mouth.

Craig frowned as he stared at the car.

Jody whistled through his teeth.

Each tire was slashed into threads of shredded rubber, cut again and again, far beyond mere destruction. Water ran from the dangling shreds like a grotesque imitation of a waterfall. Great gashes had been gouged into the body of the car, scraping through both paint and chrome.

Sylvia stood numbed while the crane pivoted in a circle and the car was lowered onto the rocky platform left open beside the pit. Then she moved forward in a queer, jerky fashion to stand beside her car, ignoring the voices of Craig and Jody, which seemed to come to her through a thickened haze.

Each section of buttery soft upholstery had been slashed and the stuffing was scattered throughout the car in sodden lumps. The dash—her fancy up-to-date dials and buttons and grills—had been beaten into submission. There was no area of her once-beautiful car that had escaped the senseless, useless destruction.

The soft conversation between Jody and Craig had no meaning for Sylvia even though her mind registered the repetition of her name. Cold heat flushed her face and burned along her veins as anger and a desire for revenge dominated all those sweet new feelings she'd grown to enjoy as she continued to stare at her car. She was remote from those talking voices in her cocoon of anger and she felt resentment toward the rough hands that shook her, the words that demanded an answer.

"Sylvia, cut it out and talk to me."

Craig's hands grasped her, and his voice demanded a response; his eyes glowed at her with some shimmering repressed emotion. Sylvia did not even try to feel what he wanted to say, but she finally let his words penetrate the shield she had thrown up.

"They have to have a positive identification."

"Yes."

"Yes, what?" Officer Daniels urged her.

"Yes. It is my car." She drew her papers from the corner pocket of her purse and offered them to the policemen. "Match the numbers. They'll be the same." Turning her back on the car, not able to bear looking at it another second, she spoke to Jody. "Let's go."

"I'm taking you." Craig spoke with a roughness that didn't quite cover his concern and led her to his car with a firm grip on her arm that Sylvia couldn't escape.

"My briefcase."

"I'll get it."

A docile Sylvia followed his lead, sat in his car seat and stared out the window as they silently backtracked down that ridiculous excuse for a road. When they arrived at her house, she flung open the car door without speaking and started to get out, but Craig grabbed her arm again.

"I want to know what is going on. Why are they after you?"

There it was again—that undefinable suppressed something in his voice. But Sylvia had no interest in Craig's secrets at the moment.

"Good question." She turned to him, flicking her green eyes over him coolly and haughtily lifting her chin. "Maybe you can tell me."

"How would I know? Did you double-cross them?"

"You have the *audacity* to speak to me in that manner!" Sylvia could feel generations of her formal Devon ancestors rising up in horror that one of theirs had been unjustly accused. "I don't even know who 'they' are." She flung his restraining hand from her, marched up her steps, and almost succeeded in slamming the door shut in his face, but Craig had matched her step for step, and shoved it back open.

"You made contact with Freddy the Hat and now they're after you. What am I supposed to think?"

"Freddy the Hat. Freddy the Hat. You keep jabbering about stuff I don't know anything about." She gave up trying to shut him out and stomped into the living room, knowing by sound that he shut the door and followed her. She turned and attacked him with returned accusations. "Who are you? And why are you in town? How did you know to be at the quarry this afternoon?" She stared at him, waiting, wanting to hear the right answers.

All she heard was the jangling of the telphone breaking into the lengthening silence between them. She reached for the phone and said a dull hello, then handed the receiver to Craig. She raised her eyebrows at him, turning her head sideways in a questioning motion of hers. "It's for you."

"I gave your number to...a friend. Said I'd be here this evening." He gave the quick explanation and took the phone, listening with a cautious look on his face that was rapidly replaced with anger. "I'll check it out."

Holding the receiver away from him like it was contaminated, Craig picked the phone base up and examined it, then threw it onto the floor with such force that the base cracked. He muttered something about amateurs.

"Are you mad! That's my phone."

"I'll buy you another one. You have an extension in the kitchen for now—but it's probably been bugged too."

"Bugged!" Sylvia stared at Craig. He was serious. How did he know it was bugged? Unless...unless maybe he had done it. And why?

Craig watched the play of emotions across Sylvia's face. Had she known it was bugged? Had they done it in case he wanted to use her phone? He was sure Roy had at least a suspicion about who he was, but was Sylvia mixed up with them or not? Either she was an innocent victim or she was the best actress he'd ever met.

Sylvia stared at the mangled phone lying in a heap on the scratched finish of her hardwood floor—he would pick the only part of the floor not covered by the rug—and thought she could hear it ringing. It took a moment for her to realize that the kitchen extension was ringing. She went swiftly to answer it and heard her mother's voice hysterically crying about her clean house becoming a shambles.

By the time Sylvia had calmed her down and talked to her father to find out what had happened, Craig had entered the kitchen and was leaning against the refrigerator, waiting for Sylvia to finish. When she finally hung up, she laced her fingers together and, making a child's fingerplay, she studied her hands carefully.

Without looking up, she told Craig, "My parents' house has been systematically ransacked." Then she looked at him, her doubt clear in her eyes. "Someone was looking for something while they were at work... and I was in school."

Desperate confusion flooded Sylvia as she considered the possibilities. Her own house had been searched gently. Then her brother had been beaten and her car stolen and destroyed. Her phone had been tapped—so Craig said. Now her parents' house had been searched rudely. *What* did they want? And *who* were they?

Looking at Craig standing so still in front of her with his arms folded against his chest, the thought passed through her mind that until she met him her life had been slowly paced, filled with normal, everyday stuff. Could Craig be the cause of all these weird happenings?

Her eyes met his squarely and he did not flinch or look guilty. Instead, a strangely gentle look caressed her and reminded her of the last night and the day before. Sweet mammoth. She had known him such a short time, yet he had become so important to her, even though she had tried hard not to acknowledge it. And his kisses... How could this big lug, whose kisses knocked off her socks, be behind all these horrid harassments?

Craig waited. He could feel her inner turmoil but he wanted her verdict to be strictly hers. She would have to make her decision to trust him without his help.

Confused thoughts raced through Sylvia's mind as she tried to assimilate all that had happened.

No. Surely not Craig. Surely she could trust him. Yes. She would trust him. She had also met perfect Roy about the same time as she'd met Craig and bought that picture for Momma that she still had to wrap.

Chapter Six

That picture. Sylvia remembered the behavior of the strange man with the old hat pulled down over half his face who had sold the picture to her. She knew that that somehow the whole crazy mess was connected with that picture, not with Craig. Just to prove it, she'd run a small test, all in the best interests of science.

"Kiss me."

Maybe Craig's eyes widened in surprise, but he was a man well prepared for emergencies and wasn't fool enough to ask, "Why?" With two strides, he had Sylvia encased in his arms, two seconds more and his mouth was asking—no demanding—from hers all that she could or would give him.

Absolute delight at the success of her test raced through Sylvia as she leaned wholeheartedly into

Craig's embrace and she gave, gave as much as he would take. Then it was her turn to demand and she took from him as she gave until their mingling could not be divided and their mouths simply gave to each other.

With a deep sigh of satisfaction, Sylvia drew her head back and smiled up at Craig, who seemed a bit unsteady on his feet. "Testing completed, Sir."

"What kind of test was that, you green-eyed she-devil? Now I'll conduct my own test."

And he snatched her to him again, but this time his hands slid down her back and his mouth probed hers until she could no longer stand alone and leaned against him for support as well as from desire. The cascading fire that came from Craig's wandering hands and leaped into her body was building, raising her temperature until she felt as if she were melting, melting into him. She had no bones, no will. It was just Craig and Sylvia and she wasn't sure where one stopped and the other began.

Then Craig pulled away and smiled down at her. "Testing completed, Ma'am."

"You . . . you big jerk. You lout. You—"

A quick kiss took away her annoyance and Craig tipped up her chin and looked down at her.

Irreverently, Sylvia murmured, "You're the only man I know who makes me feel small."

"That's good, I guess. Now—" Craig stepped back a pace to nullify the temptation to take her in his arms again and finish what he'd wanted to start. "I would like to know what brought that on."

She walked on rather unsteady legs over to the table and perched on the edge of it before answering. "I decided if you hesitated when I asked for a kiss that you were guilty of putting the bug on my phone."

He shook his head. "Crazy woman. What if I'd been too surprised?"

"Not you, Craig."

"Ever think I might have thought you did it?"

"Me? Why would I bug my own phone?"

"So your partners could hear my conversation."

"Craig." A warning note crept into her voice. "Tell me what partners you're talking about."

"I'd much rather conduct another test." Craig sauntered over to the table, seated himself in a chair and grinned up at her.

"Let's get serious."

"I am."

"Come on, Craig." Reluctantly Sylvia turned her thoughts away from Craig and kisses and more. "Now, we have to pool our knowledge to figure out what's happening." She hopped up and retrieved a piece of paper and a pencil from her desk in the corner and laid them on the table. "We can make a list. I figure it's all connected to that velvet painting I bought last Saturday."

"The one you were carrying around with you?"

"Yes. It was right after that that my house was searched."

Craig's smile vanished. "Why didn't you tell me your house had been searched? Everything kept pointing to a connection between you and the Prattys."

"Why should I have told you? All I knew about you then was that you were just passing through." And that you seemed a part of me, she could have added, but bit the words back. She wanted to keep that aspect of their relationship on hold because she was feeling too much, much too fast and Craig was still just passing through.

For some reason Craig had squirmed uncomfortably when she mentioned his passing through. Why was that, Sylvia wondered, before the second thing he said soaked in. "A connection with the Prattys as in Roy Pratty? That snake! How could I be connected with that slime?"

Craig watched her. Her hair hung gleaming about her shoulders, her arms were propped on her hips and her toe was tapping, while her eyes were glowing that strange green they had whenever she felt strong emotion. He knew then that this woman wasn't going to be one he could walk away from when this job was finished.

"Well?" Sylvia queried impatiently.

"Forgive me, Sylvia." His mouth crooked up in one corner and his black eyes were definitely laughing at her. "No one who kisses like you do could possibly have any connection with Roy Pratty."

All this talk of kissing had to stop. She already wanted far more than Craig's kisses. Sylvia pointed to the pencil and paper and frowned sternly. "If we're going to work together to figure out this mystery, you have to behave."

"I promise." Craig sweetened his grin with one of his innocent looks.

Sylvia shook her head. "Out of my mind, I am, to believe him," she muttered as she started writing a list of happenings she thought might be related.

After she had finished the list and they had discussed it, she thought about the fact that Craig had added nothing to the list, just agreed with her. He was holding something back, she knew he was. Yet he seemed as excited as she over the picture. Another piece of the puzzle missing, Sylvia pondered while she and Craig left the house to take his car to Aunt Willy's house to pick up the picture.

During their drive Craig's shrewd comments about her family's Sunday gathering started Sylvia's giggles. By the time they drove across town and pulled into her aunt's drive, she was relaxed and at ease, and had almost forgotten her Aunt Willy's obsession. But when they got out of the car and started up the walk, Sylvia mouthed a warning to Craig. She was too late.

Aunt Willy opened the door before they were halfway up the walk. The heavy frown on her aunt's face was so out-of-character that Sylvia hastily placed a hand over her mouth and faked a cough.

"'Bout time you came to visit your poor Uncle Bennett. He hasn't seen you in—"

"Three days," Sylvia broke in, knowing if her aunt got a lecture started they might be there all night. "My poor Uncle Bennett saw me at Sunday dinner." She noticed Aunt Willy was studiously looking away from Craig. The wicked sense of mischievousness that poked Sylvia couldn't be resisted.

Placing her arm through Craig's, Sylvia pulled him over to stand with her directly in front of Aunt Willy, so she couldn't ignore his presence. "You remember Craig McDonald, Aunt."

"Yes." Her aunt sniffed and pointed her nose a little higher in the air. "Indeed I do. You remember Carey Sullivan? She's getting married next month."

"That's nice, but we don't have time to chat, Aunt Willy. We've come for Momma's picture that Jody left here."

"I'll get it."

For a moment Sylvia thought she was actually going to leave them standing on the step while she brought the painting to them, but Aunt Willy opened the door begrudgingly and allowed them to enter while she went upstairs to get the picture. Uncle Bennett absently greeted them, then continued watching his television program.

In a few minutes Aunt Willy returned carrying the painting, still wrapped in the old blanket. Her arms clutched it tightly and she held it stiffly. As Sylvia reached out to take it, she spoke into the air, looking with great interest at the floor, or the walls, but not at Sylvia or Craig.

"Spoke to Father on Monday. He said sometimes the bans don't have to be read for three Sundays. Likes to perform marriages, he does."

Green eyes danced and black eyes shimmered with suppressed amusement. Craig's mouth twitched and then was perfectly still as he solemnly replied, "What a fine priest you have."

"Oh, yes." Aunt Willy brightened. "He likes babies and baptisms too, but weddings are so nice." She peered up at them hopefully.

"Thanks, Aunt Willy." Sylvia took the picture and smiled gently at her kind, fussy aunt. "We're not in the market for marriage." But as they turned to go she couldn't help thinking how nice a wedding in their small church would be with Craig waiting for her at the end of the aisle.

When Craig opened the door and lifted the picture out of Sylvia's hands to carry it to the car, Aunt Willy gave Sylvia a quick, embarrassed hug.

"Now you remember," she whispered in Sylvia's ear, "God wants babies to have two parents."

"I'll be sure to remember that," Sylvia replied dryly, as she patted her aunt's cheek and waved to her uncle, then escaped out the door following Craig, who was putting the painting into the trunk of his car.

He drove efficiently through the quiet streets of Devon and they were soon back at Sylvia's house. Craig carried the picture into the living room and propped it against the couch.

"Before we start examining this thing, there's something very important about me you should know," he said quietly.

He was so serious. What secret was he going to tell her? Sylvia waited anxiously.

The serious look on his face deepened and he placed his hand across his chest.

Was it his wound? Had it become infected?

"I'm starving."

She stared at him. The cad. Here she was all ready to hear a confession, or at least an admission of severe pain that would be serious enough to interrupt this picture-examining session, and all he was interested in was food. A smile tugged at the corner of her mouth and was answered immediately from across the room.

"My mother always told me, 'Son, never get serious with a woman who can't laugh or cook.'"

"Was that when you told her you weren't ever getting serious, even with a laughing cook?" Sylvia inquired, shaking her head at the silly look on his face.

"No. Actually, that was later. After my brother had his two kids." He was hungry, but that was a diversion. What he really wanted was to throw her down on the rug and take every piece of clothing off her while kissing every inch of her body, then make love to her so fully that she'd forget all about her pretend affair and her strict upbringing.

"Do you know that's only the second time you've mentioned your family? Why?"

Craig shrugged. "Working habits, I guess. Come on, Sylvia. You must have something to eat around here."

He had done it again. Sylvia turned away and quietly walked into the kitchen. Every time his personal life came into the conversation, Craig changed the subject. It shouldn't hurt her like this. After all, he was only a casual acquaintance briefly involved in her life. And why do I have to keep reminding myself, she asked silently as she peered into the freezer for quick food. She was a fool to hope for anything different.

Craig McDonald, you are a fool. Voices beat into Craig's head as he reflected on the slight sag to Sylvia's retreating shoulders. He hadn't missed the quick, hurt look on her face before she'd smoothed it over and left the room. But it was better for her this way—and for him too. Of course it was. She'd never be happy very far away from her family. Anyone could see that. And there was his job. She wouldn't like that, either.

"I found some Steak-ums and a loaf of bread."

The cool, controlled, feminine voice floated into the room and surrounded him with regrets. *Definitely better for you,* the little voices mocked him and reduced his rapidly decaying mood to a new low so that Craig practically stomped into the kitchen.

"I guess that's better than nothing."

Sylvia slammed the frozen package down on the tiled counter and whirled to face him. "Well, excuse me! We don't have an all-night deli in Devon and I don't exactly have time for the little housewife routine."

Why was his nose out of joint? He'd better straighten up or I'll— A slow smile replaced the resentment on her face and Sylvia ignored the warning inside her head telling her she was playing with fire. Turning her back to him again, Sylvia undid the top two buttons of her staid oyster-white blouse. She shook her head to tumble her hair about her face, slipped off her suit jacket, and kicked off her shoes.

Throwing her peach jacket over one shoulder, Sylvia turned and swiveled across the room to Craig and blinked up at him in what she imagined was a good imitation of a coquette. The astonishment in Craig's face was worth the nerve it took for her to act like this.

"Is this better than nothing?" she cooed as she pressed against him, rubbing her hand up his firm arm and becoming so fascinated with the swirls of dark patterned hair on his arm that she missed the concentrated distress on his face.

"Sylvia, don't do this."

"What, darlin'? Don't do this?" She ran her other hand up his back inside his shirt, feather light, and was rewarded as a shudder convulsed Craig's massive frame.

"The food, Sylvia," Craig muttered helplessly as she started light kisses at his opened neckline and tiptoed to work up his neck. Her open buttons revealed tantalizing flesh and the light scent she wore penetrated his flaring nostrils. She smelled like lilacs and springtime. What had gotten into her? "The picture, Sylvia." He made a last desperate attempt at reality in a heavily thickened voice before he broke.

His arms crashed around her body and he drew her to him with a force that stunned them both. "You want games? I'll play games."

But the kiss that followed was not hard and demanding, as both had expected. No, the kiss he gave her was light and filled with as much promise as a rainstorm in early April. Sylvia could feel the shimmering rainbow fill the room and she just knew that if she looked behind her she would see it. But she couldn't look. She had lost at her own game and now it was for real.

The loud, rude noise that intruded upon them wouldn't go away. When Sylvia realized her telephone was ringing, she gently pushed away from Craig and, twining her fingers in his to keep him near her, she reached out to answer it.

Her hello was met with silence. She tried again. "Hello?"

"Give . . . it . . . back." The whisper was menacing.

"What?"

"Now...or else." Seeing her face pale and her body stiffen, Craig swiftly leaned his ear next to hers.

"What are you talking about?" Sylvia asked. But the line went dead, as dead as her passion after that threat. She carefully laid the receiver down and stared at Craig. "I don't think we have much time left."

"I think you're right."

Without coming to a spoken agreement, Sylvia went upstairs to change into jeans while Craig started the sandwiches. When she returned, they worked quickly as partners, fixing a light meal that they just as quickly devoured from plastic plates while sitting at the kitchen table. Sylvia rinsed the few dishes off and stacked them in the sink.

"Picture time?" she asked Craig.

"Picture time," he agreed.

Sylvia took the lead back to the living room. Placing the picture on the carpet, she knelt and unwrapped the protective blanket and took her first look at the thing since the day she bought it.

"It looks like an ordinary picture to me."

Craig squatted beside her, his powerful legs bunching under his jeans. Sylvia swallowed and forced her eyes back to the velvet kittens, watching as Craig shook the painting. Nothing rattled. He rapped with his knuckles on the wooden frame. No hollow ring sounded.

"Perhaps the cloth?" Sylvia suggested.

"We might ruin it," he warned.

She shrugged. "I'll get her something else."

Producing a pocket knife, Craig made a careful slit along one side of the inner edge of the frame and across the bottom. Sylvia leaned forward and lifted up the cloth. Nothing there. Craig cut up the other side. Still nothing. Only a plain cardboard backing.

Sylvia settled back into a crossed-leg position and peered at the picture, guessing all kinds of wild reasons for its importance. She watched as Craig picked it up and reversed it against the lamplight to see if any hidden picture showed. Leaning closer, she frowned at the bottom half of the frame. Was that a faint line she saw? She reached out and touched the wood.

"Craig—look at this."

He flipped the picture around, barely suppressed excitment rising. "What? What is it?"

For an answer she traced the barely discernable discoloration.

"You're right. It is different."

He drew his knife out of his pocket and gently dug into the wood, finding it a different texture. "Plastic wood."

The exultation in his voice sent excited thrills through Sylvia. "What do you think is under it?"

"We'll find out." He flashed a grin at her as he carefully scraped out more of the filler. Soon a shallow depression grew and his knife hit something solid. Gently Craig pried more bits of the plastic wood out until he could see the object.

Sylvia hung over his shoulder watching eagerly.

"You take it out," Craig generously offered.

She wedged her fingers into the hole and wiggled out a key. "So this is what they're after. But what is it for? And why is it so important?"

Craig reached over and took the key between one thumb and forefinger. He turned it over and examined it carefully, looking at the number engraved on it. "Darned if I know, but it's to something, and that's what's important." He thrust it back at Sylvia. "Here," he told her. "Put it in my jacket pocket over there on the couch. We'll think about it later. Right now I want to get this picture back the way it was."

Sylvia pushed herself up and walked over to the couch to pick up Craig's jacket. She reached down, thinking how sturdy and tough the denim material was, much like its owner, but when she lifted it, one side sagged and an unexpected weight pulled at her arm. Stuffing her hand into the generous pocket, she found her fingers sliding into a hidden slit and fitting around a sleek piece of metal, like a gun. Withdrawing the object in her hand, she stared at the deadly little machine.

Her voice came out in an odd undulating manner. "Craig? In your pocket?"

Immediately he looked up and saw her staring at her hand as if she held a viper in it. "Careful, Sylvia." He leaped up and gently took the weapon from her as she stared at him as if he were a total stranger. "It's all right. It's for my job and I have a permit."

As though that made it all right. Sylvia slipped her hands into her own jean pockets and dropped the key into the left pocket. Why would he need to carry a gun and why was it loose in a hidden pocket? Didn't they always wear holsters under their coats in the movies?

"I thought you were a businessman," she whispered, with a scared look on her face. "What are you?"

Craig gave a small sigh, for such a big man, and the expression on his face was unhappy. She was thinking exactly what he'd thought she'd think. Well, it couldn't be helped. "We haven't time now to talk. Let's get this picture taken care of."

So he still wouldn't tell her. An obstinate look shadowed Sylvia's face and set her mouth in a firm line. If that's the way he wanted it, she wouldn't ask again. It didn't matter to her, anyway, she tried to convince herself. Releasing the key her left hand was still clutching in her pocket, Sylvia turned toward the kitchen and side door to the garage.

"I have some plastic wood out in the garage left over from fixing some old nail holes in the back windows." She looked past Craig as she moved around him and spoke to the wall. "I'll get it."

"Do you have any good glue?"

"Yes."

"We're gonna need some for the fabric we cut."

She removed herself from the room in search of the two items, wondering why it was so important that they put the picture back together. She had just found the glue and dug out the plastic wood from a cardboard box of odds and ends when Craig opened the kitchen door and called into the garage.

"Sylvia, do you happen to have an old key that you don't need anymore?"

"There's a box of old keys around here somewhere."

"I need one. See if you can find it for me."

"Okay. Here's the glue."

After more tugging and moving forgotten items around on the shelves in the rear of the garage, Sylvia found the keys. She picked out one that wasn't rusted at all and took it into the house with the plastic wood.

Craig had finished gluing the velvet to the backing so professionally that Sylvia could scarcely see any difference at all. "That's very good." She couldn't resist saying, "You're a man of many talents," and stuck her tongue in her cheek, pushing it out at him.

He looked up in time to catch the glint in her eyes and grinned at her, relieved that she had momentarily forgotten that she was upset with him. He much preferred a teasing Sylvia to a hurt and bewildered Sylvia.

"I'll show you more of my talents later."

"Do tell." She spoke coolly, but her heart began to beat faster as she remembered some of his marvelous talents.

"Here. Put your key into the hole and we'll cover it with your plastic wood."

"Won't whoever put it there know the difference?"

"Sure, but it may buy us some time."

Kneeling beside Craig, Sylvia slipped the replacement key into the depression and he hastily filled the area with the fast-hardening wood substitute, packing it in solidly, and smoothing the surface to match the contour of the picture frame.

"All done."

"Now what?"

"Now we leave it propped right here to finish drying and we finish our other business."

Sylvia scrambled to her feet at the dark gleam in Craig's eyes. "I really think you should be going now. It's getting late and I need to go to bed."

The gleam in his eyes intensified and Sylvia could have kicked herself. Why did she have to use that choice of words?

"Now that's an interesting invitation."

"It was not. Now you go back to your motel room."

"Oh, Sylvia. That's not nice." Craig rose, dusted off his jeans, and began moving toward her. "Motel rooms are dingy, lonely places."

She backed toward the door into the entryway. Craig matched each movement with one of his own, as if he were cautiously stalking nervous quarry, which was exactly what Sylvia felt like.

"Craig, no." She tried to inject a forbidding warning note into her voice, but only succeeded in emitting a breathless, wishful sound as she bumped up against the umbrella rack in the hall and watched him approach.

Her green eyes began to glow as she stood unmoving, just waiting, backed against that foolish umbrella thing. Craig felt the thudding impact of that glow starting low, deep within, building, tightening. How he wanted her. Her. His thirty-year-old, pretend-affair, single English teacher. His green-eyed she-devil, with the fire lights in her hair.

The beating of her heart was timing her short, even breaths as Sylvia's defenses ebbed under his midnight gaze. When Craig stopped in front of her she held herself still, keeping her hands from quivering only by clasping them behind her. One of his hands wound through her hair and held out a handful of the glittering mass, which sparkled with the colors of moonlight on fire—a wanton shimmering that brought sparks to those dark eyes. The feel of his rough hand mingling with her hair sent myriad little shivers through her body.

As his other hand tipped her chin up, her mouth went soft in anticipation of his kiss and at the sight of her waiting lips, Craig lost his control. He hit the light switch for the hall and living room; then, sliding his powerful arms around and under her, he picked her up easily and began to mount the stairs, while his mouth took hers and he fenced with her tongue savagely. This time there would be no games, he promised himself.

At the top of the stairs, he paused long enough to ask, "Which room?"

"End of the hall, to the left," Sylvia whispered from near his shoulder. Doubts began to rise within her.

Shoving the half-open door with the back of his shoulder, Craig moved into the room and placed Sylvia on her bed.

She made a motion to rise and he sank down beside her. "Wait, Craig." *This shouldn't be happening. Dear God. How can I bear it if he makes love to me and leaves? How can I bear it if he doesn't make love to me and leaves anyway?*

"Forget it, Sylvia. Forget all those cans, and ifs, and shoulds you've been brought up with. It's just us and what we both want."

Sylvia's good intentions along with her inhibitions began to melt away under the heat of spiraling desire as Craig quickly had her blouse unbuttoned and began to worship her body with the movements of his practiced hands. Quick gasps came jerking from her throat as she lay under him, and her head turned from side to side, seeking surcease from the splendid torture of his tongue over her cheek, down her neck, and down... She caught at his head.

"Craig, no," she whimpered and smoothed her hand across his cheek as his searching mouth caught and stayed.

There was only her and Craig and...and a small thump downstairs that vaguely registered in the back of her mind, as she touched and caressed his roughhewn face. Another tiny scraping sound intruded from below. Reality intruded into Sylvia's passion, cooling her response.

"Craig, I heard something downstairs."

Craig felt her swift withdrawal and silently cursed the reason. His cool logic, which he depended on for his job, had fled him tonight. "Ignore it," he urged her, wanting to break the neck of whoever or whatever was responsible for this disastrous turn to his smoothly progressing evening.

A sharp breaking sound followed by a loud oath caused Sylvia to jerk upright. Clutching her blouse together she opened her mouth to call out, "Who's there?"

Chapter Seven

Craig swiftly covered her mouth with his wide palm as a deadly silence reigned downstairs. "Shhhh," he cautioned.

He had that too-patient tone parents often use with errant children and Sylvia didn't like that at all. She fumbled with her buttons and glared at him as he pulled his shirt down. A muted rumble of voices drifted up the staircase in the quiet house.

"They're downstairs."

"Well, of course, someone's downstairs," she whispered. "That's what I tried to tell you."

"*They*, Sylvia."

"You mean they, as in the picture, the search, the—"

"Yes, with us trapped up here. Listen."

And she heard it. The heavy footsteps had found the front stairs in the dark and were beginning to climb. Sylvia bit her lip and tried to breathe deep slow breaths to counteract her thudding heartbeats.

Craig slammed his fist into the soft bedding. He looked at her in apology, his mouth a straight slit, and said in that low urgent voice, "My gun is downstairs in my jacket. I hope there's not too many of them to fight."

Springing to her feet, Sylvia quoted softly, "He who runs away, lives to fight another day," and tugged at his arm. "Come on."

The hesitant footsteps were halfway to the top of the stairs.

When Craig merely looked at her with a puzzled frown, Sylvia got behind him and pushed. "Move it, you big lummox. Let's get out of here. This way." She darted swiftly down the hall in the opposite direction from the threatening steps climbing the main stairs and touched the opening to the hidden stairway. The door swung back and she whirled into the safe zone, grabbing the rail with one hand and beckoning to Craig to follow.

"Nice," he whispered, raising his eyebrows and sliding in behind her. As the door swung shut he whispered, "Did you have smugglers in your ancestry?"

She rolled her eyes in exasperation and, realizing he couldn't see her, tapped her finger on his mouth. Craig promptly sucked on it and, catching her around the waist whispered into her ear, "Never, never put your finger on my mouth—it gives me ideas."

Sylvia jabbed him in the stomach with her elbow and was rewarded by a soft whooshing sound. She grinned. Somehow the danger of those thugs in her house was relieved by Craig's presence, but she knew that the stairs might be found if the search was thorough enough and that she and Craig were not really safe yet.

Edging slowly down the dark, narrow stairs, Sylvia pulled at Craig's hand to show him she was moving. Hand in hand they eased down the steps to the kitchen. Before opening the door, they listened carefully.

Voices and footsteps were moving through the house. They could hear three of them—covering both exits and one in the garage, too close to the basement stairs for them to be used.

Opening the downstairs door, Sylvia tiptoed and placed her mouth next to Craig's ear. "Follow me." As she tugged on his hand in the darkness and he moved noiselessly behind her, Sylvia gave an inaudible thanks to her grandmother for putting in the wood elevator, and cautiously darted the short distance to it. Thank goodness the floor didn't squeak.

She felt for the power switch at the trap door and activated it. The door slid open and the wire cage sitting just under the floor vibrated mutely.

"I think it will hold us both."

His crooked grin flashed at her in the dim light and he answered in a muffled voice, "If you're game, I am."

"Hurry," she whispered urgently as the door to the garage rattled. "Get in. I'll push the down button and jump on."

Craig coiled his long legs under him in the heavy wire box. A few sticks of wood left in the bottom of the box dug into his leg muscles and he shifted uncomfortably. Sylvia punched the green button and dashed for the shaft. As the box began to move slowly down the heavy framework, she jumped, landing on top of Craig. A tangle of arms and legs filled the box and Craig's solid body cushioned Sylvia as she squirmed to sit up.

"Stop wiggling against me. You're causing problems," Craig whispered.

Sylvia instantly stilled her struggles, thinking the short ride down was much too long to spend pressed against Craig. Much too long. When the wood elevator clicked into place at the bottom of the shaft, she breathed a small breath of deliverance and hopped out.

Carefully she sought the downstairs buttons and pushed the up one, causing the slight humming of the elevator to resume as it began to move slowly upward. They waited by the elevator until it clicked into place at the top of the frame and the efficient motor shut off.

Just in time.

Lights flooded the upstairs as the intruders found the switches.

"Can they find the elevator?" Craig asked.

The stumblings had ceased. Now the heavy footsteps were walking firmly around her house while the men searched.

"Maybe, if they look hard enough. But I don't think they will—I hope not," she added with a shiver of doubt.

"Listen to the pigs. They're not even trying to be quiet."

It was true. She could visualize the brightly lighted rooms from the dim light seeping through the nooks and crannies of the old house. They had turned on all the lights and the voices coming through the floor were muffled only by the strength of the house.

"But they should have found the picture by now."

"No." Craig couldn't help letting smug satisfaction creep into his voice. "I slid it under the couch against the wall before we went upstairs. They're still looking for it."

"I hope they don't decide to look down here." Her remark reminded them that they still needed cover, so they edged behind the high piles of firewood stacked in the corner.

It galled Craig to be so helpless while those coyotes sniffed around above him. And there was Sylvia. She wouldn't be hiding down here in her basement while those crooks ransacked her house if it wasn't for him. And she shouldn't be. No woman should have to put up with such a situation. What wife would want a husband who did these things routinely?

When Craig realized the track his thoughts were running on, he almost snorted aloud. *Husband and wife. Now look where you left your mind. She may be one classy lady who can handle adventure, but she's not looking for a husband any more than you're looking for a wife.* And he wasn't looking for a wife at all. No sir, of course not. Nothing permanent for him. *Then why are you so concerned about her safety?* Because she's a human being, that's all. *Sure.*

The effect of this internal dialogue was to cause Craig to crouch down and lean against the wall, refusing almost sullenly to allow himself to look at Sylvia and most certainly not to reach out and touch her, which seemed to be what he most wanted to do. Instead he concentrated on reciting to himself all the reasons he could think of for not getting further involved with this woman.

Sylvia had her own problems to think about and didn't even notice Craig's preoccupation. She scooted backward to the wall on her seat and leaned against it beside Craig, trying not to listen to the racket coming from above them, first in one area, then another of her house. Her skin crawled as she thought of them touching her things, fouling them with their nasty fingers. Sylvia shuddered and moved closer to Craig.

When her arm rubbed against his, she felt him jerk and scoot away slightly so they were no longer touching. What in the world, Sylvia wondered. Was he regretting his involvement in this whole deal?

If it hadn't been for her, he would be doing the work he came to Devon for and getting ready to leave. With a feeling of regret she told herself that it would be better if Craig stayed away after this night; a few more uninterrupted minutes and the pretend affair would have been a real one.

A naughty smile sneaked about her mouth as she contemplated how nice it would have been, but—the smile vanished—she would have paid for it when Craig left and never returned. Her grandmother's voice seemed to sound in her ear: *"You play, you pay."* Sylvia closed her eyes and Gran seemed so close, in the old cellar that had been the foundation of her house for so many long years. *How much, Gran—and is it worth it?* Thoughts of her and Craig together in her bed upstairs haunted her.

She knew she should be ashamed of herself with the trend her thoughts were taking. But she wasn't. Craig's long legs were bunched uncomfortably behind the sticks of wood, and her eyes kept straying to their knotted muscles straining the fabric of his pants.

Loud excited yelps filled the upstairs and carried clearly even through the massive timbers of the house.

They must have found the painting, Sylvia thought. They sound like a bunch of hyenas finding a dead carcass. Footsteps thudded across the floor to the front door, then there was silence.

Crouched on the floor, Craig and Sylvia waited, listening for sounds of the men. The possibility that the silence was a trick to get them out of their hiding place occurred to Sylvia, and she nudged Craig, quietly, sharing her thought. A quick nod from him showed he agreed with her, but his manner was still quiet, and even cool, toward her.

The silence upstairs continued. So did the silence in the basement between Craig and Sylvia. Finally Sylvia scrambled to her feet and headed for the stairs.

"I'm going up now."

"No, wait." Craig unfolded and stretched. "Let me check it out first."

"By all means."

Either he didn't hear the sarcasm in her voice or he ignored it. Pushing the button, he waited for the wire mesh box to hum down, then climbed in, gesturing for Sylvia to start the elevator climbing. As the box slid up the shaft, Craig tried to tell himself that it would be easier to just finish the job and move on, rather than considering the alternatives.

Sure, that's why all you can think about is getting into her bed.

That has nothing to do with the future, only a passing attraction.

Right.

It seemed to Craig that he had never been so frustrated and confused since he had been fourteen and watched his nubile next-door-neighbor sunbathing in her backyard.

The wood elevator locked into place and Craig cautiously eased his head out of the hole and surveyed the room. No one there.

Bending down, he turned to tell Sylvia, "I think it's clear." But she wasn't there. "Sylvia?" Where was that woman!

A clear chuckle came from across the kitchen floor. Craig snapped around and saw two sparkling green eyes peeking at him from behind a door tucked in an alcove next to the door to the garage.

"I came up the easy way."

Craig struggled to control his temper as he uncoiled himself from the wood box while Sylvia sauntered over to the trapdoor.

"Having problems?" She smiled sweetly at him.

"No!" He lifted one brawny leg over the edge of the side and heaved himself upright, stretching to his full height. "Don't you ever follow orders?"

"Rarely. And stop bellowing at me; it's not polite."

"Why didn't you wait until I checked things out?"

"Because it wasn't necessary. I came up the stairs to check for myself."

"I was checking first!"

"You're still yelling at me," Sylvia observed mildly, not bothering to tell him that she could yell with the best of them, if she felt like yelling. Looking at Craig's flushed face and clenched fists, Sylvia had a flash of intuition. He hadn't wanted to be first; he was upset because he'd wanted to protect her and couldn't. His male ego was dented and she'd scraped it even further by ignoring his need. How sweet. "If I promise to let you check the rest of the house first, will you promise not to yell at me again?"

Craig closed his eyes against the pull in those sea-green eyes before he drowned in them. *Holy smithers! If you don't get out of this town soon, you're a goner. Maybe too late, even now.* He opened them again, controlling his agitation with an effort. "I promise."

And he smiled—that lazy smile of leisured evenings and sharings—then turned to enter the living room.

Good grief, Sylvia. The man has s-e-x written all over that smile and you just stand here and drool. I'm cool. I'm very cool, she kept assuring herself as she trailed behind him, flipping out some of the lights the men had left on during their search. She turned out the overhead light in the living room, which left on only the ornate cast-iron floor lamp in the corner by the couch. Then, feeling she was once again in control, she turned to observe Craig.

He was on his hands and knees peering under the couch. "Yep, she's gone." His firm derriere was tightly outlined as he bent over.

Sylvia rolled her eyes in supplication and muttered to herself, "Yep, she sure is," but her meaning was entirely different. To keep her eyes off his smoothly moving frame as he uncoiled to stand up, Sylvia wandered over to the couch and picked up Craig's jacket. The peculiar weight was gone. She wedged her hand into the inner pocket. "Craig—your gun's gone."

"Perfect. Just perfect." He took his jacket, a disgusted look on his face, and felt his pocket as if his gun might magically appear when he touched it.

"At least they don't know we have the key," Sylvia said, attempting to console him.

"Not yet."

The flat, matter-of-fact way Craig spoke sent a shiver through Sylvia. What would they do when they did find out? They wanted that key badly and Sylvia had it in her pocket. Her hand slid down and touched it. What did it fit? A treasure chest? A locker at the airport with dope in it?

A string of furious expletives from Craig interrupted her reverie. She looked up at him and widened her eyes innocently.

"You really should watch your language," Sylvia rebuked him mildly and was rewarded by watching his eyes close and a muscle twitch in his cheek as he clamped his square jaws tightly together. She watched fascinated as moments passed before he opened his eyes and glared at her.

"Oh, dear," Craig mimicked in a falsetto voice. "I am so sorry to tell you the key is now gone. Please excuse my lapse into vulgar language."

Stifling a gurgle of laughter, Sylvia gravely inclined her head to him. "I will manage to overlook your transgression this one time provided it never happens again."

In the same shrill voice Craig replied, "Oh, goodie." Then he whirled around and slammed his fist into the wall. "I was so close," he roared, "and now the infernal key is gone."

"Will this make you feel better?" She dangled the key between her thumb and forefinger high in the air at his eye level.

Two swift strides brought him to her side. He jerked the key from her fingers and held it up to the light. "This is it." Snatching her to him and giving her a violent squeeze that she thought would surely crush her bones, Craig said in a pleased voice, "That's my girl. How'd you do it, Sylvia?"

"By putting the key into my pocket instead of your jacket—Craig, I'm dying."

He grinned at her and loosened his bear hug, but one brawny arm still held her against his chest. With his other hand he searched blindly for her pocket, his eyes fixed on her face, as he felt for the opening and plunged his hand into the depths of her jeans. "Here. You keep it. It's safer with you."

The feel of his hand moving deep inside her jeans pocket caused flutters to work up from the center of her body and ripple outward until Sylvia leaned limply against Craig for support.

Her head had dropped back and he could see that her green eyes were fogged and her mouth was opened breathlessly. The excitement of relocating the key vanished and Craig felt his own breath tighten as Sylvia's special charm wrapped around him again. Taking her parted lips fiercely, Craig allowed his senses the nourishment of her taste, the fragile smell of the fragrance she wore, the ultimate feel of her curves and hollows pressing against him.

Forgetting his recent vow of temporary celibacy, he slipped his hand out of her pocket and slid it beneath her bottom, turning her and lifting her into his arms. "Sylvia," he groaned as he cradled her, lowering her to the floor. "I can't leave you alone no matter how hard I try."

With her body aching for him, and her cheeks flushed from emotions she had felt only with him, she felt more sexy and desirable than she had known she could. "Craig." Her hand smoothed the tortured frown on his forehead, as the truth tumbled from her lips. "I don't want you to leave me alone, not ever."

The words hovered in the air between them, then the tensing of his muscles ran right through her and Sylvia wanted to bite a hole in her tongue.

"I didn't say that."

Craig sighed. "I wish you hadn't." He released her and sat up, avoiding her eyes. She was so warm, so giving. How could he put her aside and walk out? *You'll be leaving as soon as you find the stuff, you jerk. You have no right to take anything from her.*

Feeling brittle, as if she might break into a million pieces, Sylvia sat up and stiffly rose to her feet. Sweeping her arm up she pointed to the door. "Out. Just get out."

"I'm not leaving you here by yourself tonight."

"You are not staying here!" Her voice rose with each word.

"Be logical, Sylvia. They might come back if they check for the key tonight."

"I don't want to be logical. I won't be logical. I—want—you—out—of—here!"

Craig planted his feet onto the carpet and stood up, crossing his arms across his chest, his face implacable. "Listen, Sylvia. Let's leave our personal feelings out of this. You could be in danger."

In danger. Dear God, yes, she was in danger. From him. And he stood there talking so calmly about leaving personal feelings out of it.

"The only danger I'm in is from you!" She hurled the accusation at him, thrusting her chin stubbornly upward. She didn't care if she was being unreasonable. "You come into my life and think you can pretend to have an affair with me and fool my family. Well, you don't fool me one bit."

"As I recall, you're the one who asked me to start this charade of an affair." He suppressed his own temper, feeling her hurt and knowing he was responsible for it.

"You're being logical again." Hands on her hips, she glared at him, blinking her eyes rapidly. Whirling around and presenting her back to him so he couldn't see her misty eyes, she asked, "Why did you have to come to Devon? I was happy before I knew you."

"Sylvia—don't." He took a step toward her and stopped. He couldn't take much more. His stomach hadn't felt this bad since that summer he'd had an ulcer. But she didn't stop.

"I can't stand it. You blow hot, then cold. You kiss me then put me aside...." Her voice broke and she stopped, feeling great sobs building up, like the night her grandmother had died. And she felt like someone *had* died—the new Sylvia, who had been coming alive in Craig's arms. Tears started to streak down her face, first slowly, then faster as she could no longer control them. Silent heaves shook her shoulders.

"Are you crying, Sylvia?"

"No!" A loud sob hiccuped from her throat. "I never cry."

"Ah, Sylvia, you said you didn't want a real affair." Then his logic deserted him and Craig stepped forward, yanking her against him again.

"No, no, no." She beat her fists on his chest ineffectually then collapsed again him crying, burrowing her head into the material of his shirt and grasping its lapels as though she'd never let go, mustn't let go, or she might fall and never rise up again. She clung to her rock, her mountain, and shuddered with her sorrow until the tears could no longer come.

The feel of his broad hand stroking her hair continued to soothe her as her tears finally softened and slowed. She was afraid to look up at him, afraid of what she might see in his face. After telling herself, *Hey, you're a Perkins, chin up*, she leaned back her head and stared up at him. There was no mistaking the pain in his eyes.

"Sylvia, I—" He started to speak, but she quickly placed her hand over his mouth.

"No, don't say it, I understand. You're a wanderer. I'm a stay-at-home. It's all right." She managed a smile to prove that she was correct. "I've had a couple of bad days and I'm overtired from last night."

She moved away from him and wandered around the room, touching the lamp shade and straightening a magazine before she flashed him another bright smile. "Sorry I made your shirt soggy. I don't usually do that. Be right back—I'll get blankets and a pillow for you to sleep on the couch."

Craig stood helplessly, letting her chatter sweep over and around him, brushing away those sweet desires each knew the other felt but neither was willing to bring up again. It was better this way, he tried to convince himself. Keep it on a business level. His eyes followed her feminine shape as she moved swiftly through the doorway, then his ears listened for her light footsteps as she ran up the stairs. The sag of his broad shoulders spoke of more than tiredness and the new lines across his face added another ten years to his age. There was no room in his life for romance. No room at all.

Chapter Eight

Early morning light battered Sylvia's eyes as she blinked sleep from them. A wide yawn accompanied by long stretches almost finished the job of waking her up. When she swung her legs over the side of the bed and sat up, a sharp ache jabbed behind her ears, and the woman who stared back at her from the mirror had puffy eyes and limp greasy hair. *Serves you right for crying into your pillow half the night.*

When she stood up, the pain made a circle around the back of her head. She cringed and decided that there was no way she was going to be able to go to school to face her students. Mr. Lord was just going to have to get a substitute and that was that. Sylvia made it into the bathroom and ran a tubful of hot water, then lowered her body into the steaming water and sat for ten minutes. After she washed and rinsed her hair under the shower, she returned to her room to brush it while blowing it dry. Thank goodness I have a simple hairdo, she thought fifteen minutes later, when her hair once again looked clean and alive.

Feeling almost human again, she quickly donned fresh jeans and a mint-green pullover to combat the chilly morning air. Sylvia slipped the key into her pocket and bounced down the stairs, determined that Craig would be amazed at how cool and distant she would be. No more crying jags for Sylvia Perkins. No sir. She would be calm and reserved. No emotional outbursts.

Slowing the bounce in her step, in case Craig was still asleep, Sylvia peeked into the living room and saw the past night's bedding neatly folded and laid to one side on the couch. She poked her head in farther and found Craig sitting in her favorite wing chair with a new phone held to his ear. His voice rumbled into the telephone as he ended the conversation and hung up the phone.

"Who was that?" Sylvia asked as she came into the room with all her good intentions.

"Your principal."

"You called my principal?"

"I didn't think you'd feel like going in today so I explained to him that after the events of the past two days you were in no condition to teach. He agreed and doesn't expect you in until tomorrow."

"You mean he didn't even complain about getting a substitute?"

"Wel-ll—" he flashed a crooked grin at her "—he might have had a few words to say on that subject—until I told him where to go to find one."

"You didn't!"

"'Fraid so."

A giggle bubbled up as Sylvia thought about the expression on her principal's face when given that direction. "Craig, you're terrific. When I think of the times I wanted to say that, but never dared—" She held her arms to the ceiling and spun around. "Ta Da. So I'm sick today?"

"Definitely. Mentally ill, most likely."

She stuck her tongue out at him. "Probably from my association with you."

"You win, green-eyed devil. Now can I borrow your shower?"

"As long as you don't take it with you."

"Ouch. Bad, Sylvia. Very bad."

She smiled at him. Dancing flecks of sunlight caught by the crystals hanging overhead shimmered in her hair and skipped across her smile. The world started to stop for Craig and he almost told her why, right then, but she turned to pass into the kitchen and the moment vanished, and the spinning merry-go-round that Craig was riding speeded up and went on.

"Have a nice shower," she called back to him.

"Yeah, sure," Craig mumbled to himself as he clambered up the stairs. "Sure."

Remember, be cool, she told herself as she hurried into the kitchen. If she had stayed and exchanged quips with him much longer, she might have forgotten her resolve. He was so funny, and gentle, and strong, and— Enough! Get busy fixing breakfast, Sylvia, and forget the catalog.

As she busied herself with the cooking, events from the night before kept sliding through her mind. It was all the fault of the key in her pocket. What was it for? There was something about it that looked familiar... if only she could remember.

Sylvia felt the gentle warmth of the old kitchen stove radiating out as she passed it on her way to the gas range. Figuring Craig had started the fire, she decided to use it. She poured the egg and cheese mixture into the hot cast-iron skillet and began to stir.

If only he were from Devon, or at least somewhere nearby. She had so many ties to this place—her job, her family and her house. Her relatives might drive her nuts at times, but all the shuttling around she had done as an army brat gave her strong feelings of belonging to the Perkins-Martin clan even more power. Putting it most simply, this was home.

Dumping the cooked eggs onto two plates, she opened the door to the warming oven hanging over the wood cookstove and put the plates into it. Her always comfortable old house felt even more homey with the knowledge that Craig would soon be down to eat breakfast with her. Craig. The bitter with the sweet. Soon he would no longer be in her life at all. That's the way it has to be, she reminded herself fiercely, now forget it and enjoy his company. The toast popped and she turned to butter it, spreading the yellow goo carefully out to the edges, holding her lips tightly together just in case they wanted to tremble. Which they didn't. Definitely not.

Reaching up to the top shelf for the good juice glasses, Sylvia saw the cobble-patterned sugar bowl her grandmother always used to keep her treasures in. Again something nudged her memory. She took down the bowl and lifted the lid. Stirring the contents with her finger, she saw it. A small key almost exactly like the one in her pocket, with just the edges different.

Her smile widened and spread across her face as she looked at the key in the bowl. Just wait until she told Craig! As if her pleasure in her discovery drew him to her, she heard his footsteps moving on the back stairway, then the door opened and his presence filled the kitchen, surrounding her with another kind of warmth. His neatly combed hair was still wet and his scratchy beard shaved off, and—his shirt was gone.

"Hope you don't mind, but I used your razor."

"No, of course not." *Don't just stand there staring, Sylvia.* Her fingers clutched the antique sugar bowl and her body sagged against the base cabinets.

"There oughtta be a law," she muttered as she took in Craig's bare feet and ran her gaze up his snug low-cut jeans to that tempting display above his belt line. Didn't he even have on shorts? Whoever said that men didn't have curves had never viewed such a muscular panorama.

Sylvia could not remain unmoved at the sight of all that lovely flesh. Her fingers twitched to touch and stroke, and she tightened them out of sheer desperation. The metal object clutched between her fingers gouged her hand. She welcomed the call back to the mundane and forced herself to look away from Craig.

"Go up and get dressed, then we'll eat."

"You needn't be so huffy." Craig scowled at her. "I haven't any more clothes here."

"In the third bedroom on your left going up the back stairs. Jody left some stuff in the closet. It might not be your style, but it's clean and it'll cover your body." *Then I won't have to look at it!*

"Yes, ma'am!"

Craig stomped back up the stairs grumbling to himself, then Sylvia could hear him banging around in the bedroom. After the noise subsided, she tried not to imagine him taking off his jeans before he redressed. Instead she busied herself setting the table and pouring the juice. Just as she placed the warmed plates with the eggs and toast on the table, the back stairs door opened once again.

Is that supposed to be an improvement? Sylvia's mouth fell open and she almost moaned aloud. It was going to be very hard today to keep her mind calmly on business.

This time Craig was fully dressed in Jody's clothes. The height was almost perfect, but Jody's frame was more angular than Craig's meaty bones. Sex appeal oozed from every skintight inch of his borrowed outfit.

"Better?"

Better? And how! But she didn't dare tell him that. "Much better," she managed to mumble aloud before she snapped her mouth shut.

As Craig walked over to the table, Sylvia took ten deep breaths, and told herself how calm and cool she was. When she spoke again, it was in a low, well-modulated voice.

"I do hope you slept well last night."

He gave her an amused glance before sitting in front of the heaped plate of food. "Fine. And you?"

She started to glare at him and remembered her resolve. She smiled faintly, like a calm and refined lady should. "Quite well, thank you." Picking up a bite of eggs, she chewed in silence while she waited for him to initiate a topic. Instead he seemed content to devour the breakfast she'd fixed. At least he could comment on the food, she thought crossly. "Nice weather today, isn't it?"

"Mmm" was the noncommital answer.

Sylvia tossed her fork onto the table. Her green eyes glinted across at him. "Talk to me, Craig!"

"Now that's my Sylvia," Craig responded with satisfaction. "That other cold statue was someone I didn't know."

"I was trying to be cool and calm today," she said in a disgusted tone.

Craig leaned forward across the table toward her. "Forget cool and calm. You were made to be full of fire and warmth and... spirit...." His words trailed off as their eyes met and held.

The intensity in his face and the darkness of his eyes swallowed up the reply she tried to make. Sylvia's mind went blank and her limp hand slid off the table onto her lap, striking the hard key in her pocket. The key. Desperately she clung to that thought and drew away from the ever-shrinking threads weaving rapidly between them. She couldn't let them grow. She wouldn't.

She cleared her throat twice before she could speak. "Craig, I've figured out what the key goes to."

He was silent for a moment, then abstractedly asked, "What?"

"I think I know what the key fits."

She had his interest now. A quickening excitement lightened his eyes. "What?"

"Grandma always kept her valuable papers in a locked drawer in her old rolltop desk. This key looks almost exactly like the one to Grandma's desk."

"Oh, terrific." Craig leaned back with a disgusted look on his face. "And where are we supposed to find the desk it fits? Knock on everyone's door and ask to check out their antiques?"

"So I didn't think that far," Sylvia said, making a face at him. "Anyway, it couldn't be in just anyone's house."

Listlessly she slumped in her chair, stirring the milk into her coffee as she glanced out of the window. She knew the air outside was cool, but the sun shone so invitingly. After the cold winter, the cool spring day was almost balmy. Just the right weather for long drives.

Long drives. Sylvia straightened in her chair. What was it that man at the truck had said? *I've heard its nice this time of year out on old Barlow Road.* "Craig, listen to me."

As Sylvia explained about the cryptic sentences of the old man, Craig's interest grew. "I think you might have something there, Sylvia. Let's take my car and check it out."

This time as they walked out the solid wood door, Sylvia turned and locked it behind them.

"It's about time," Craig said. "If you had locked it last night maybe we wouldn't have had our visitors."

Sylvia started to reply sharply that she'd never had any unwelcome visitors before and had left her door unlocked many times, but her attention was attracted to the curtains across the street that were drawn back on one side, giving them a curious lopsided effect. A short, dumpy figure was barely discernible standing beside the window.

Sylvia chuckled and climbed into the car. "Mrs. Winegath is spying on us."

"Do we care?" Craig asked as he slid behind the wheel of his nondescript blue car.

"It wouldn't do us any good to care—she's obsessed with neighbor watching." Sylvia waved in the direction of the window and had the satisfaction of seeing the curtain drop abruptly.

Minutes later they were driving along one of Devon's bumpy back roads, peering at each house they passed. As they drove farther from town, the houses grew farther and farther apart and were more dilapidated and the roadside growth grew more tangled and wild. Twice they stopped to check out houses that were obviously not occupied. The doors hung askew and the windows were all broken or boarded up, but they found no furniture, not even a stray pot in the kitchen.

Sylvia grew discouraged. "If there was a desk for this key, it may be gone by now."

"Let's drive on a little way," Craig suggested. "He must have had a reason for mentioning this road. It sure isn't the scenic route."

For another two miles they followed the narrow road without seeing another building or passing a single car. Then they saw an old house tucked between dead and dying elm trees.

Craig whipped his car into the overgrown driveway with a screech of his brakes. Bushes brushed the sides of the car as he stopped by the front door. "Your friendly neighborhood Halloween house," he quipped as they stared at the sagging roof and boarded-up windows while the wind whistled through the bare branches of the dead elms.

"The door looks locked. How are we going to get in?" Sylvia asked.

"No problem. First we check the windows. If they're all boarded, then I'll unlock the door."

"You have a key?" Sylvia cocked her head and looked at Craig. First a gun, now a lockpick?

Craig swung open his car door without answering her question. "Coming with me?"

She accepted his challenge and slid out of the car. As they pushed through the growth around the side of the house, Sylvia was glad she had worn jeans. Slacks would have been ruined. They checked all the ground floor windows, but all were tightly boarded, and the second floor windows were too high to reach, so they returned to the front door. Craig took a small black kit from his pocket and turned his back on Sylvia, but she saw the tiny pieces of metal he used as he worked on the lock.

Moments later Craig pushed open the door and peered into the house. Sylvia followed him closely, not wanting to be left alone. Craig shut the door behind them and they stood for a few seconds to get used to the darkened interior. Ghostly white shapes, which Sylvia quickly identified as furniture covered with sheets, loomed in the room about them. They began lifting each sheet to look for a desk. There wasn't one in the living room, nor any of the other rooms downstairs.

"Let's try upstairs," Craig suggested.

They edged up the central stairway, careful to keep to the wall, in case the bannister was weak. As they neared the top of the stairs, the light from the unboarded upstairs windows increased until they stood in full light at the top of the stairs.

"You take that side of the hall. I'll look in the rooms on this side," said Craig.

Sylvia nodded reluctantly. She wasn't at all crazy about the expedition. Methodically she moved down the hall and opened doors to dusty rooms that obviously hadn't been used in ages. There is no desk, and even if we find one, there will be nothing in it, she told herself as she pushed open a door to an empty room filled with bookshelves. Well, not quite empty. Here and there lay a few volumes left behind, dusty and tumbled in a heap. And in the corner was a rolltop desk, almost identical to her grandmother's.

In the stillness of the room, Sylvia tiptoed over to the desk and checked the only drawer that had a lock. Slipping the key from her pocket, she slid it into the keyhole and turned it, then tugged at the drawer knob.

It pulled open. A small metal box nestled in the drawer. "Craig!"

The sound of running footsteps neared and Craig burst eagerly into the room. "Did you find it?"

Sylvia poked at the box. "I waited for you to open it."

Craig grabbed the box in one hand while he fumbled with the catch with the other.

Sylvia tapped her foot impatiently on the floor and stood with her hands on her hips, elbows out in defiance. "Just one minute, Mister McDonald."

Craig's head snapped up and he lifted his eyebrows at her stance. "What?"

"Before you open that, I want to know just who you are and what this is all about."

A deep sigh escaped Craig as he looked at her flushed cheeks and stubborn chin pointed into the air. "It's complicated."

"We have plenty of time. No one's going to bother us here."

"I promise I'll tell you, but after we open the box."

"Oh, all right." Sylvia begrudgingly gave in, unwilling to admit that she was just as curious about the treasure in question as he was.

Carefully unlatching the catch, Craig turned it gently and lifted the lid. They stared into the oblong metal container.

A piece of paper.

All that was in the box that they had been through so much for was an ordinary piece of notebook paper folded in half. They stared at each other and she could see the disappointment in his face.

Sylvia plucked the paper from the box and opened it, a perplexed frown marring her brow. Her long fingers smoothed the crease and she studied the series of squiggles and lines on the page before her, dimly conscious of Craig's scrutiny over her shoulder as the lines gradually began to make sense to her. It was a map. But what for?

"I feel like a kid looking at a make-believe map for buried treasure," Sylvia said as she glanced up at Craig. "Any idea what this is all about?"

"Yes." Craig carefully eased the paper from her grasp and laid it on the desk. Hunching over it, he traced the area outlines of the unknown spot. "And this probably *is* a treasure map—if we can figure out where it's located."

"You're kidding." She stared at him, fascinated in spite of her recent desire to throttle him.

He anchored the paper with the long edge of the box and leaned back against a wall, his hands shoved into his pockets, his black eyes memorizing her features. "I think it's about time I told you a story."

Sylvia lifted one hip and rested it on the corner of the desk, folded her arms across her chest, and waited for Craig to continue.

"About thirty years ago three men robbed one of the biggest banks in New York City. They hit it just right and made quite a haul, walking away with about ten gold bars and two million dollars."

Her eyes widened and a small whoosh of breath whistled past her teeth.

Craig nodded in response. "Quite impressive, isn't it? The bank thought so, too and, unwilling to trust just the police, hired a team of investigators to help find the men."

"And you were one of them?"

He flashed a grin at her and quipped, "I know I look old, but surely not that old." Then he went on more seriously, "I was hired more recently because the last of the robbers was being paroled. Although the robbers were caught six months after the heist, the money was never found."

"They didn't spend any?"

"Not a penny." Craig's gaze slid away from her face and he fixed his eyes on the ceiling. "Two of the men died in prison, the third was paroled last month. His name is Jerry Pratty." He still wouldn't look at her.

The significance of the name slowly sank in. Her mouth fell open at least a foot before she snapped it shut. *The rat.* The unadulterated, unmitigated, unprincipled *rat*, Sylvia fumed. "And what relation is Roy Pratty to this Jerry Pratty?" Ice couldn't have been colder than her voice was, and one foot began a staccato rhythm against the wood floor.

"Son. And the man who sold you the painting—you must have given them their code by mistake—was Fred Pratty, his brother. He's a petty con man, involved in dozens of schemes, but never convicted. Also known to cops as Freddy the Hat, because he always wears one." Craig eyed Sylvia's restless foot, nervously tugged at his tight jeans and wondered why he was babbling on so. Did he really think he could delay her inevitable reaction? One quick glance at her face shouted "no" at him.

"Why—I repeat, *why*—didn't you tell me all this to begin with? It would have saved us all a great deal of trouble."

Now he was even more nervous. She wasn't going to like his answer at all. "Because . . . I . . . I thought that you might be . . . one of them."

"You what!"

Immediately Craig's defenses went up. "Now, Sylvia, look at it from where I stood. You were friendly with two members of the Pratty family. You lived in a big house with a new car, fancy jewelry—all far beyond a school teacher's salary. I didn't know if I could trust you or not. I had to find out."

Sylvia's anger dribbled away and was replaced by sheer misery. All this time he had been using her, watching her to see if she had connections with the Prattys. "I really helped your plans along when I asked you to pretend to have an affair with me, didn't I?"

An acrid taste coated her mouth and she drooped all over. "I bet you laughed, every time you kissed me, at what an easy target you had this time." She twisted around and stared at the blank wall, wishing the room was bigger so she could ignore his presence better.

"Ah, no, Sylvia. Please believe me." His big hands grasped her shoulders and gently, but forcibly, turned her around to face him. "It's true that I didn't plan on what happened between us. At first I only wanted some fun, but then...things changed and I didn't want you to get hurt."

She looked up at him, searching his face for the truth, wanting to believe, needing to believe, but wary of allowing herself to believe. One hand reached up and drew back, then rose again and touched his cheek. "Truly, Craig?"

Craig shook her shoulders slightly then slid his hands down to find her wrists and captured them, her sturdy bones seeming small in his even larger hands. He touched her nowhere else. Only his hands around hers, his face tilted down to inspect her countenance, but she could feel him with every inch of her mind.

With a set jaw and a rough voice he answered, "God help me—yes."

A half smile struggled to form on her face and faded as she tried to think of something witty to say to lighten the atmosphere and could not. "It's all right, Craig. You were just doing your job."

"Not where you're concerned, Sylvia. Believe me, my feelings toward you go far beyond doing a job."

Did she dare hope that he felt as much for her as she did for him? But there was still the matter of him going and her staying. A little catch in her breath drew his attention as well as her own.

"Sylvia, you're not going to cry on me?"

She had to chuckle weakly at the look of horror on his face and a totally unexpected solution sprang into her head. Could she really do it? No, impossible. Why not? Put it on the back burner and let it simmer, ole girl. Think about it.

The mixture of fleeting expressions on her face fascinated Craig. He couldn't stand it when she cried, so when no tears came, his panic dwindled, but her next words were unexpected.

"Come on, you big lug. We have work to do." Sylvia picked up the map. "First, we find the loot, then, second, we have a long talk together. Agreed?" She propped one hand on her hip, dragging his hand with her movement, and tilted her head to one side, a soft siren smile on her lips.

Her sudden change of mood puzzled Craig, but the rush of relief he felt that she no longer blamed him for keeping secrets from her left an uneasy feeling. Why did her opinion matter so much to him? It went beyond not wanting her to be hurt. But he didn't dare dwell too much on why.

"Yes—" he nodded solemnly "—we have work to do, so let's get started." Reaching to hold the map with her, he said, "We need a reference point, anything to pinpoint the location."

Sylvia studied the map, her head so close to Craig's shoulder that it was an effort to keep from leaning over and resting on its warmth. Her other hand was still innocently twined with his and a tinge of— No, she wouldn't let it interfere. It was work time. Down, girl, she scolded herself. As she stared at the squiggles and lines on the map, they began to take on a definite form. Somewhere she had seen that shape before. Now, where?

Reaching out with a finger, her brow drawn down in concentration, she traced the dark lines, skipping the queer zigzag pattern and concentrating on the outer perimeter. Her finger quivered as realization sunk in. The stimulation of discovery sent her calm facade flying and animated her entire body.

Poised as if she were ready to soar away, and her face glowing with anticipation, she swung Craig's arm wildly. "That's a map of Devon: the whole township, not just the village!" She trailed her finger along the border.

"You're sure?"

"It's not very plain, and certainly not to scale, but I'm sure of it. It resembles the markings of the big Devon town map Richard has in his office."

"Richard?" He didn't like that affectionate tone in her voice. "Who's Richard?"

"A friend." Still peering at the map, she missed the dark look he gave her. "Richard Allen, the district game warden. His office is next to the sheriff's. We should take the map to him. Since he's an expert on the area he could pinpoint the exact spot where this smaller zigzag area is located."

"Is he married or single?"

"Single. What has that got to do with—" She stopped abruptly as she caught the scowl on Craig's face. "I don't believe this. You're jealous."

"I am not."

"Oooh, huffy, huffy."

"I am not!"

She giggled delightedly. "You are too, but you needn't be. Richard is a very good friend and I'd dance at his wedding any day, but his bride I won't be."

Craig mumbled something through his clenched teeth.

"What did you say?"

"Nothing," he muttered.

"You did too."

"I said: that's good, then I won't have to smash his teeth in," he roared at her, and stared as she doubled up laughing. "You have a strange sense of humor, Sylvia Perkins." Craig couldn't help feeling disgruntled at his confession; after all, she didn't have to laugh.

Sylvia rose on tiptoe and planted a firm kiss on his cheek. "Silly mammoth, I can't believe you're jealous. Come on. Let's get his expert opinion."

Craig returned the empty box to the drawer and reluctantly followed her out of the room and down the gloomy stairs, watching without comment as she carefully folded the map and put it in her deep jeans pocket. He was still miffed by the realization that he was jealous, and even with her reassurance, he was still annoyed at the affectionate tone she used when speaking the game warden's name.

Chapter Nine

Craig drove up in front of the long wooden frame building that Sylvia directed him to, and parked the car on the first try in the only spot left. *There. Let Richard Allen beat that!* Then he grinned at how foolish he sounded, even to himself.

"Why the big smile?" Sylvia asked.

"Can't tell you." He shook his head at her. "It'd spoil my image."

At that she wrinkled her nose at him and slid out of the car with the map held tightly in her hand. Craig matched her stride for stride and they walked in rhythm up the cement steps and around the corner of the building, pushing open the double doors in unison. Up three more steps made of thick pine, then they continued down a dim hallway, oppressive with the heavy smell of dust and old wood. Three doors down, Sylvia stopped and knocked.

The man who opened the door wore a light brown uniform with patches on his sleeve proclaiming him to be a member of the state of Maine's game warden service. He wore L. L. Bean boots and a gun rested in the holster around his waist. His face lit when he saw who was standing in his office doorway. "Sylvia! What brings you here today?" He looked with interest from Sylvia to Craig and back and asked, "Is this a holiday I missed?" as he stood aside to let them enter the room.

Sylvia introduced the two men, noting that they eyed each other almost as warily as Craig and Jody had the first time they met. She sighed. Richard must have heard the latest gossip.

"We need your help, Richard." She unfolded the map and spread it open, pushing aside the clutter on his desk to make an empty space.

As Richard viewed the sketchy map, Sylvia told him as much of the story as she felt comfortable telling, with Craig thawing out enough to put in a few comments to make her story more clear. It was obvious to Craig that there was no sexual interest between Sylvia and Richard and that their relationship was more one of the brother-sister type, but he was determined to make the point to Richard that Sylvia was his, so he placed his arm around her waist and kept it there, leaning over the map with them.

"Looks like these squiggles are located here." Richard walked over to the wall and pointed a pencil eraser at the printed Devon topography map. "This is the old Devon cemetery. It hasn't been used since it was filled up during World War I." He looked back at the crinkled paper. "I'd say that zigzag is the stone wall boundary on the north side."

"That's it!" Sylvia hugged first Craig, then Richard. "We know where it is. Now all we have to do is get it."

"Sounds like more fun than I've had in months. Mind if I go along?"

Sylvia looked at Craig and waited for his answer.

He hesitated only for a few seconds. "Sure, Allen. We can use an ally, but we'd better go now."

"I'm ready." Richard grabbed his personal communicator and started toward the door, followed by Craig and Sylvia.

As they arrived at the car, a series of beeps came from Richard's caller. He gave Sylvia a disgusted look and switched it on. After the exchange of a few sentences, he flicked it off and shoved it back in his belt.

"Got to check out a call on poachin'. Can you wait?"

Craig slowly shook his head. "We'd better not. They'll be desperate when they find the key is gone—if they haven't already."

Sylvia gave a little shiver. The deciphering of the map had helped her to forget about *them*. "Come catch up if you get back before we do."

With a lift of his hand, Richard was off in his truck down the road. Sylvia and Craig piled in Craig's car and left on the opposite road. Once again, Sylvia gave Craig such precise directions that he never had to hesitate at a single turn.

The old curving road wandered past abandoned farms with fallen barns where lilacs grew wildly, released from the housewife's pruning shears, and masses of flowers spread from once carefully tended beds. There was both beauty and sadness in viewing the riotous color in the decayed acres of a once-thriving farmstead. Sylvia thought it was an appropriate road to lead to an unused cemetery.

"There." She spoke quickly and pointed up the long gentle hill.

Craig jerked on his brakes and looked. The narrow road was a single lane between two rows of trees and eased halfway up the hill.

"Should we walk from here?"

"No. Drive up. There's a small turnaround space where you can park."

He shifted the car and turned into the road, driving slowly over the deep ruts up the hill to the parking place. After getting out of the car, they stood together, uncertain how to proceed.

The small, unenclosed graveyard was filled with tombstones amid swaying broad-leaved ferns. Two giant pine trees near the edge of the plot towered above a broad dry-stone wall, spreading their thick branches to shade the rocks from the sun, and leaving the sunken graves to soak up the warmth.

"It seems so still. There's not even any wind," Craig commented.

"Maybe they know we're here and are waiting."

"The Prattys?" Craig jerked his head around to stare into the surrounding forest.

"No," she whispered. "The people in the graves."

Despite the thin chill that chased up his spine, Craig scoffed at her. "Nonsense. Let's go try the wall."

They carefully walked around the depressions in the ground and the occasional fallen tombstone. Sylvia stopped at one set of three large and five small headstones.

"Look, Craig. This man lost two wives, one at twenty and one at forty. Five babies died under three years of age, and he lived to be seventy." She looked accusingly at him. "The wives probably died in childbirth."

He threw up his hands in surrender. "Not my fault."

"You're a man, aren't you?"

"What kind of logic is that?"

"Why does it have to be logical?" She lifted a disdainful shoulder and continued to the outer stone wall, leaving a muttering Craig trailing behind her.

When they arrived at the wide pile of stones, Sylvia looked closely at the peculiar zigzag pattern on the map. First she scrutinized the layout of the wall, then she paced down to where she thought the pattern began. "Here, I think."

"No." Craig paced off the distance and ended two feet farther down the wall. "His legs might be longer than yours. Let's try here."

She shrugged and started helping him shift the rocks. Some were light and they laid them aside in a small pile, but some were huge and they strained and tugged together to roll them off the pattern. Sylvia broke three fingernails and Craig smashed his hand trying to lift an extra-large rock by himself, but after they removed the first layer the wall still looked the same, only flatter.

Sylvia gazed at the endless stones and grimaced. "Are you sure anything is here? Maybe that map was meaningless."

"In that case, why did they try so hard to get the key back?"

She had no answer, but her hands hurt and her back ached, and the physical exertion had made her sweaty all over. She felt dirty and grimy as she sat down on one of the rocks they had moved and blew a stray lock of hair out of her eyes. "Now what?"

"We try another layer."

With a groan, she heaved herself to her feet and began to push at another rock while Craig pulled until it toppled over and slid off the wall.

"We could get sent up for vandalism, if we don't find anything."

"Trust me."

I want to. I really do. She thought the words at him, but they had nothing to do with treasure and rock walls. Did she dare to trust him wholeheartedly? If she could, the course she was contemplating might be workable after all. Gradually another layer of rough gray rocks peeled off the wall. After the fourth rock in that layer, Sylvia noticed several flat pieces of slate underneath.

"Craig, look. Isn't this peculiar? Slate in a rock wall?"

Excitement lit his face as he studied the variation. "It must be under the slate! Dig, woman, dig!"

Generously refraining from reminding him that they were not digging, Sylvia tugged at the rocks with renewed enthusiasm, but she could not keep up with Craig's vigor. He seemed to glow with an energy charge as the rocks tumbled from the slate base to drop to the ground below.

When all the slate was uncovered, Craig eagerly leaned forward and reached for the largest piece. He hesitated, as if afraid he would only find more rock, then picked it up. The slate was interlaid over other slabs of slate. Sylvia picked up the remaining pieces in that spot and an area of darkness appeared. Craig feverishly plucked the slate from all along the marked line to expose the gaping black hole inside the stone wall, then plunged his hand into the space.

At first he felt nothing except the sides of more rocks, then, all the way at the bottom, he felt something different, a brick shape, several of them almost buried in the dirt. He dug them out, one at a time, and handed the oblong blocks to Sylvia without looking at them.

Disappointment filled her as she took the dirty bricks and stacked them in a pyramid. All that work and anticipation for bricks? Maybe, she thought, they're covering up the real thing. Craig was still reaching for something.

It was smooth and cold, with pointed edges. Craig felt it with the side of his hand on the bottom of the hole. He reached deeper, groping around the edges. It felt like a metal box. He tugged at it and rocked it back and forth to loosen it from its long resting place and eased it upward into the sunlight.

It was bigger than he'd thought at first and a little rusty, but he was elated as he held it aloft to show Sylvia and he felt filled with the pride his ancient ancestors might have felt in bringing home their war prizes.

"We got it!"

Bending over eagerly to look at the box, Sylvia eyed the rusted lock. "How can we get it open?"

"We'll take it with us. Maybe break it open at your house just to make sure the money is in it before I call anyone."

"Well, at least we found part of it. These things—" She picked up a red brick in disgust and threw it against a large rock. Chips of red brick flew off and landed on the ground. "That brick isn't very hard," she commented and picked it back up to look at the broken corner.

A dull golden sheen winked back at her, reflecting the overhead sun. Excitement rushed through Sylvia. She ran her finger under the thick red coating, cracking and breaking off more of it to expose the yellow underneath. "Craig! These bricks are gold!" She was actually holding a bar of solid gold—and standing over more.

They grinned at each other like a couple of monkeys pleased at finding a lost bunch of bananas.

"We did it." Craig laid the metal box carefully at his feet and reached out his hands to Sylvia. She dropped the bar, onto grass this time, and stepped into his arms, hugging him tightly.

The thrill of the find acted as a catalyst for their ever-present attraction and the fire simmered over as their need for each other overcame their reluctance to make commitments. The haven of Craig's arms felt like home to Sylvia and she pressed her curves against him, wanting to be still closer. She wanted to feel him, to taste him, and reached up to pull his head down to her parted mouth.

Sweet. So sweet. Craig knew that always afterward the scent of lilacs would bring memories of Sylvia. He didn't care; he wanted to remember her. Who was he kidding? He didn't even want to leave her. Maybe there was a way to work things out. Maybe he could—He'd have to think on that one, he decided as he took her mouth and gave his in return and his arms tightened across her back.

Wishing she could stay forever in his arms, Sylvia let her fingers creep between the loosened buttons on Craig's shirt and eagerly touched his chest. She wouldn't give him up. She couldn't. But—the timing wasn't right for now. The vague sense of forboding that had been with her since they'd arrived in the cemetery came between them and she gently pushed Craig away.

A frantic breeze sprang up and a chill feathered across Sylvia's skin. *Get out. Get out.* The need was urgent to leave the place, with all the dead bodies and broken dreams that surrounded them.

"Quick, Craig. Let's get this stuff into the car."

Catching her sense of urgency, although not understanding it, Craig followed her lead and they made swift trips to carry the loot back to his car, each trip getting faster until they were panting in their haste. After Craig unlocked the trunk to his car, they bent and lifted, bent and lifted, stashing the bars and box inside the trunk and pushing the lid tightly shut after they were done.

Just as they climbed into the vehicle and slammed the doors, Sylvia caught a flickering glimpse of movement through the tree-lined lane. She turned and froze. A battered truck was moving slowly along the narrow road to the cemetery. The truck from which the paintings had been sold.

No words would come. Silently she pointed in the direction of the truck and her breath came in a strangled gasp. Craig turned to look at her and when he saw the expression on her face, followed the direction of her pointing finger. The truck was still edging along the rough road, blocking it, pointing inevitably in their direction. Craig turned back to Sylvia and she nodded mutely.

He swore savagely.

Sylvia didn't bother to comment on his choice of language; she felt the same way. Just when they had found it, the creeps had found them.

"Any way out of here?"

"Just that road."

"What's over the hill?"

She looked at him with interest. "One of the main roads is at the bottom of this long hill to the left. To the right is three miles of forest."

"Hang on."

Sylvia clung to the seat, hope flaring in her at what he meant to try. Jerking the gears into reverse, Craig turned sharply and aimed the car up the hill behind the cemetery. Maybe the gang didn't know they were there. Maybe they could get over the hill and down the other side to the highway before their enemies spotted them.

Swerving rapidly back and forth, Craig dodged the car between the trees. Sylvia drew back from the open window as flailing branches slapped into the car and the pungent odor of bruised evergreens filled the car. A startled grouse whooshed from its hiding place as the fleeing couple bumped over the uneven terrain.

Only a short distance until the top of the hill. We're going to make it, Sylvia thought joyfully, when a savage shout rose from the truck below them. A cold dread reached deep into her body and her mind, gripping her with unknown fear as the echoing call was repeated. She closed her eyes and willed Craig to go faster.

Craig pressed his foot against the gas pedal as hard as he dared and he twisted the car back and forth with his powerful arms. But the car was too large for many of the narrow spaces and hunting for a passage was taking too much time.

Rage boiled inside him at the danger in which he had placed Sylvia and at the impossible situation with which he was faced. Him. Craig McDonald. In all his years in security work, he had never allowed himself to get trapped before.

The car began to bump erratically in his grip even though he was clutching the steering wheel tightly. Oh, no. Despair shot through Craig as he realized they'd blown a tire.

Spinning sideways at the top of the hill, the car graded over a boulder and skidded into a gnarled pine standing sentinel among the spruce and fir.

As the car lurched into the tree, Craig's head snapped backward then forward, hitting the wheel. The sound of gas drizzling out of the tank and dripping onto the leaves of the forest floor trickled through the fuzziness in his head. The last thought in his mind was of how polluted the ground would be, then a black mist closed over him.

Why did we stop, Sylvia wondered wildly as the car halted suddenly. We've got to get moving. She opened her eyes and saw Craig draped limply over the steering wheel. "Craig? Are you all right?"

As she leaned over to shake him she saw three men with guns running toward them. A quick wash of fear swept across her and she froze as they surrounded the car. Then she remembered Richard and relief brushed through her. He would be coming to look for them. They only had to hang on until Richard came.

"Git out, little lady." The picture seller opened her door and motioned to Sylvia.

What was it that Craig called him? Freddy the Hat, she remembered as she stumbled out the door and held on to the side of the car as her head spun furiously. The name fits, Sylvia thought as she stared at him. The hat he wore now was different, but just as battered as the one he'd had on when she'd bought her mother's present.

She heard Craig being issued the order to step out on the other side of the car and her eyes searched the ground for a stick with a vague idea of using it for defense.

As if knowing her thoughts, a sneering voice warned, "Don't even try it."

Glancing up to find Roy Pratty standing next to her, Sylvia glared at him before turning her head away in disgust. "Don't think you can get away with this. People know where we are."

His answering laugh was harsh. "Look at me."

She tilted her chin up and stared him in the face. A large purple bruise around his right eye advertised his wrestling match with Craig and his perfect features looked twisted and ugly.

"Do you think you can get away with this?" Roy gestured toward his eye.

"Serves you right for what you did to my brother."

Roy snorted. "That was supposed to have been you driving that car. It was his own fault he got beat up. He shouldn't have tried to fight us."

She stared at him. "You are sick. You—"

At that moment Craig rounded the corner of the car under guard of a third man whom Sylvia had never seen before. As the other two kept their guns on Craig and Sylvia, Roy slapped his hands up and down Craig's hefty muscles, seeking and finding his pocket knife.

Craig's cheek muscle twitched. No other visible sign existed to show he was perturbed. He stood still, his broad shoulders slightly hunched, hands down along his sides. Only Sylvia saw the glow in his midnight black eyes.

When Roy turned back to Sylvia, he smiled mockingly at her. He leaned close to her and ran his eyes slowly over her body. "No weapon on this one," he called to the older man.

Craig swayed beside Sylvia. I won't fall, he promised himself. I won't fall.

"You're in a peck of trouble, Miz Perkins." Roy's oiled voice rolled over her like a snake.

Sylvia shivered and her stomach tightened as she shrank back from him.

"Leave the girl alone," the controlled voice of the third man interrupted. "Your poor judgment and lack of planning has caused us enough trouble."

"Me?" Roy whined to his father. "I didn't give the key to her."

"You will mind me with no back talk. Is that clear?"

Each word was quietly spoken with a hidden edge to it that was instantly obeyed. It was clear who was the leader and Sylvia knew this man was the dangerous one, despite Roy's vulgar threats. She sensed the movement beside her as Craig's self-control faded and his body wavered in reaction to the head blow he'd received in the car. Sylvia moved defiantly to him, slipping his arm around her neck and propping him up with her shoulder.

Another nasty remark from Roy was covered by a muffled command from his father. Roy obediently turned away from them but cast a look of hate at Craig behind his father's back. "This way," he muttered sullenly, and turned into the deep woods.

Jerry Pratty motioned his gun towards Roy's back. "Follow him."

"He can't walk far," Sylvia pleaded, her shoulder beginning to ache under Craig's heavy weight.

"Then we'll drag him. Get movin'."

"Craig, please listen to me. Try to walk," Sylvia frantically whispered to him. A rush of relief shot through her when his weight shifted and his legs began to move in the direction that she tugged him. The sag of his usually erect shoulders attested to his groggy state, but his feet kept moving. Sylvia tried to dodge the branches that Roy whipped back in his haste, but while trying to protect Craig's face, she missed one and it whacked her across the right cheek, leaving a stinging line from her nose to her ear.

It was obvious that Roy had been through the path before and she could see the occasional cuts in the trees that he depended on for markers. Someone will find our car and come looking for us, she thought, desperate for a piece of hope, and they can follow this trail too. She looked from one small slash ahead to the next one several feet away.

"Don't count on it, lady." The confident voice spoke behind her. "I planned this part, when my intelligent son kept messing up and I had to come out of hiding. As soon as we take care of you two, we'll get rid of your car and my money, long before anyone comes looking."

The sinking sensation Sylvia felt was definitely not due to the fact that they were going downhill. *Take care of you two.* Those words had a hollow, ominous sound, but she determined that she wasn't going to let them see how disturbed she was. She was a Perkins. Up went her chin and her mouth tightened. Craig's weight was numbing the arm with which she supported him, but she was determined they'd get there standing up if it killed her.

Propping up Craig and following Roy, ever aware of the two men pacing behind her—and their guns—Sylvia stumbled along, sometimes barely catching herself in time to keep from falling. The woods grew denser around them and in the thick shadow of the trees, mosquitoes buzzed and landed to taste her blood. She slapped at the piercing bites with her free hand, wondering how much farther they would be herded and what was going to happen when they arrived there. It seemed to her the very trees held their breaths wondering about their fate as they checked the passage of the wind.

The hands on her watch showed that only thirty minutes had passed since the nightmare had begun. Craig was standing up straighter by now and bearing most of his weight. Once he had tried to whisper a question to Sylvia, but an ugly poke from the nearest Pratty gun stopped his attempt.

A small clearing opened up in front of them, exposing a hunting camp tucked in the edge of the woods. Roy walked directly toward the camp, so Sylvia knew this was their destination. The relief she felt was tinged with distaste for the isolation of the place. Several bricks had tumbled off the chimney and lay in a scattered heap on the roof, but a shiny metal stovepipe sticking out of the roofline testified that the camp was not abandoned even though the building appeared to stare vacantly at them out of the boarded windows.

As they moved closer to the camp, Sylvia could see holes in the roof where shingles had been blown off in the winter storms and not yet replaced by the camp's absentee owner. The board on the top step to the porch looked rotten.

Roy stepped carefully over the rotted wood, and Sylvia urged Craig to stretch up when they reached the same spot, which he did with ease. He was also noticeably lighter on her supporting shoulder, so she knew his recovery wasn't just her wishful thinking.

Jerry produced the key to the padlock for the front door from his pocket and unlocked it, leaving the lock hanging on the door frame as he kicked open the swollen door. Roy stood back this time and made Craig and Sylvia proceed in front of him, grinning inanely as Sylvia curled her lip in disgust at the condition of the interior.

Dim light leaked in between the boards on the windows, showing the broken inner panes of glass. Shards on the floor crunched underneath their feet as they entered and echoed loudly in the nearly empty room.

Sylvia caught a glimpse of a kitchen through an open doorway at one end of the long room. Double bunks built into the wall near the unused fireplace were matched against the opposite wall in the narrow room. The fat, black heating stove squatted in the center of the room. When she was shoved closer to the bunks Sylvia could see that thick dust lay on the sheets.

Good grief. They're going to put us on that dusty bed. Over and over, during the thirty seconds it took for the Prattys to march Sylvia and Craig to the two bunks opposite each other, Sylvia kept telling herself, *I'm a Perkins. I'm a Perkins.*

Jerry Pratty picked up a roll of rope and proceeded to tie Sylvia's feet together and her hands behind her back. At that sight Craig went crazy, and it took both Roy and Freddy to hold Craig down and then all three to lift and swing him onto a bunk after he was tied. Sylvia heard the solid thunking sound as he slammed into the wall and she cried out, "Craig!" as she tried to twist away from Jerry's renewed grasp to see Craig.

"Take a nap, sister," Jerry commanded her and he dumped her facedown onto a bunk on the opposite side of the room and left her.

The dust filled her nostrils and a spasm of coughing racked her chest, covering the faint sounds of retreat. Jerking her head away from the bed she clamped her lips together hard to choke back the coughs. For the next five minutes she struggled to overcome her coughing spell, then the quiet of the camp sank in.

Sylvia swung her head left, then right. No Prattys. "Craig?" she whispered, twisting to look across at him lying quite still in the awkward position in which he had been thrown. Oh, God. Was he— She couldn't even think it, but two blows on the head within thirty minutes? She had to get to him.

Rolling over with her hands tied behind her back took more effort than Sylvia had thought it would, and the pressure on her arms as she rolled onto her back hurt. Realizing that she was at the very edge of the bed, she sat up carefully and swung her bound legs over the side of the bunk.

How did one walk with no leg movement? She tried rotating her body from side to side. That got her a few inches across the space that separated them, but the floor was too rough. She could hop, she decided, but after three short hops she wavered and lost her balance, falling onto the floor on her side and banging her left elbow.

"Ouch," she yelped from her lowly position. Then she had the bright idea of rolling over to Craig's bunk. Swing, push, roll. Swing, push, roll. It was dusty, rough and splintery, but she gritted her teeth and finished up against the wall next to him. Now to get to her feet. She placed her bottom against the wall and pushed herself up inch by inch, until she was standing over Craig. "Craig? Can you hear me?"

A slight movement of his head rewarded her anxious query and she eased onto the skinny bunk beside him.

"Sylvia?"

His voice was groggy but it sounded wonderful to her. "Craig, darling." The words slipped out unnoticed by Sylvia. "I was so worried." Still unable to check his face, she nuzzled her cheek against his back.

"I made a real mess of things."

"Don't say that, Craig. It just happened."

"It wasn't supposed to." His voice was clearer now. "I've got to get us out of here before they come back." He raised his head weakly then dropped it back again.

"Don't try to be so macho. You're not responsible for everything."

"I am for this fiasco," Craig said as he struggled to sit up.

"Will you stop it! Even if we could get the lock off a locked door or these boards off the windows, how could we get out of the forest? You can't even sit up." She shoved him back down on the bunk. "Just rest for a while. Then we'll try to escape."

Craig had no choice but to give in. The throbbing in his head receded to a nagging ache when he lay back on the mattress, and he tried to think of a course of action that might work. It was unthinkable to have Sylvia at their mercy—and his job honor was at stake.

"Craig?" Her whispered voice carried a different note this time. "Do you think...they will...you know?"

"Kill us?"

"Yes."

"Not for a minute." Nor did he really think the Prattys would kill them. Robbery was one thing, but murder carried too many problems for them. But there *was* his job to consider.

If he flubbed up this one and let them get away again with the money, he might as well quit. And Sylvia. He knew he must look like a boob to her, getting her stuck in this. I'll make it up to her when we get out of here, he vowed.

Resting against Craig's broad back, Sylvia wondered if his reassuring words had been only for her benefit. Briefly she considered getting up and hopping around to check out the cabin; she might be able to find an old knife or something in the kitchen to cut the cords. A yawn broke from her as her eyelashes fluttered against her cheek. Lying with Craig, she felt so secure, like nothing bad could ever happen. In that moment of truth she admitted that she loved him. And she swore that if they made it out of this mess, she'd never willingly let him go. *I'll follow him anywhere, even if it means leaving Devon and my family and my house.*

The strain on her body from lack of sleep and stretched nerves betrayed her and she floated into an uneasy dreamworld where she jumped from treetop to treetop, looking for Craig, always moments ahead of a nameless monster that shook the ground with thunderous stomps. Jerking herself half-awake, Sylvia found herself lying curled against Craig on the dirty bunk. As she slowly came back to consciousness, the pounding on the door began again.

Chapter Ten

After the knocking subsided, Sylvia heard muttering voices and her heart beat faster as a fresh touch of fear brushed her. Her first thought was: *They're back, and we're still tied.* Her second was: *Why are they knocking?*

One voice lifted and was recognizable. "Sylvia? Craig? Are you in there?"

It was Jody! She barely had time to wonder how he had gotten there and to poke Craig when she heard Richard's voice calling to demand an answer. Oh, joy! Reinforcements.

Sylvia sat up and shouted at the door, "We're here and we're all right."

"Stay away from the door. I'm going to shoot the lock off," Richard replied.

"No problem." Sylvia chuckled. It would have taken her twenty minutes to hop to the door anyway. "Craig." She shook his shoulder. "Did you hear?"

"Yes," was the quiet reply. He knew he was being foolish, but Craig was disappointed that he wasn't the one to put that excited note into her voice, that he wasn't the rescuing hero. It was then that he decided that never again would she be exposed to the dangers of his free-lancing profession.

The report of the gun thundered through the small cabin, then the door swung wide open to let in a patch of sunlight. Jody stepped in first and glanced quickly around the main room. Calling to Richard, he dashed over the floor to the prisoners, cutting their tight ropes with a sharp hunting knife. At first, Richard lingered near the door to assure himself no one heard the shot, then he, too, came to help them stand up.

It was a lot harder than Sylvia had thought it would be. While she had lain there, the constricting ropes had slowed her circulation and her limbs were half numb. And how was Craig? She looked to him anxiously.

Craig hated the drugged feeling he had from the ropes and the knocks on his head. While he could sit and stand alone, it was with an effort, but he'd be darned if he'd let Sylvia support him again.

"Can you move?" Richard glanced toward the door again. "I want to get out of here before they get back. They might have heard the shot and decide to investigate."

"What about the money?" Craig demanded.

"That can wait. We can get the sheriff to help us."

Craig couldn't deny the logic in that statement, but he wanted to, and would have, except for Sylvia. He wanted to get her out of there and then he'd settle with Roy and the others.

They hurried toward the door. Sylvia was limping and Craig was commanding his head to straighten up. *Hurry* was the unspoken word hanging in the air urging them on.

As they clustered together outside on the creaky porch, Sylvia heard the sound of a motor chugging along the unused logging road that ran past the camp. A chill coursed along her sluggish veins, speeding up her circulation tremendously.

"Craig, what if it's them?" She moved against his side, clutching his arm.

"Let's hit the woods and scatter. They can't find us all," Jody said.

"But we might be easier victims separated than together," Richard volunteered.

"We should go back into the cabin and wait for them," Craig said, as the sound of the truck drew closer.

"Are you crazy?"

"What? We'd be sitting ducks!"

"I say listen to Craig."

Craig's breath caught at the look of confidence Sylvia gave him. No one had the right to that much trust. What if he was wrong and flubbed again? It would work; it had to. "Here's my plan." Rapidly he laid out for them what part each would play.

Sylvia snatched the door open and as the others reentered the cabin, Craig stopped to yank off the broken lock before shutting the door firmly behind him. Richard gave them a wink and a victory signal then strolled through the open doorway into the kitchen and vanished around the corner. Jody flattened himself against the wall behind the door, totally hidden in the darkness of the room.

With Jody and Richard out of sight, Craig turned to Sylvia and draped his arms around her waist, tugging her toward him. "I could be wrong. If this doesn't work..."

His eyes were so serious that she smiled up at him. "It will work," she whispered to him in reassurance, loving the feel of his arms around her, his clasped hands firm against her spine. *It will all work,* she wanted to tell him, but couldn't get the words out.

The steady throb of the truck motor was very close now. Craig led her to the bunk where Jerry Pratty had left her.

"It won't be for long," he said, as if he could read her mind, and he leaned down to touch his lips to the corner of her mouth, and when she closed her eyes with a sigh, he deposited two light kisses on her eyelids. Kisses to seal a promise—one that he made not aloud but to himself. Touching her scratched cheek gently, he asked, "Does it hurt?"

"Not much," she insisted in spite of her grimace at his touch. "Not nearly as much as my ankle after we almost went down over that rock."

So brave. And so beautiful. Even with the scratches and disheveled clothes and messy hair. He lifted her hair from her neck and combed his fingers through the tangled thickness, her nearness blocking away his awareness of the roar of the approaching truck.

"Oh, Craig," Sylvia murmured and reached up to brush his lips with hers, letting her hands wander up his back and stop at the nape. When Craig's mouth sought hers desperately, she clung to him, as heedless of the outer world as he.

"Will you guys stop puttin' on a show," Jody hissed at them from his vantage point by the door. "They're here."

There were sounds of slamming truck doors, a muffled shout, and arguing voices coming closer.

Sylvia gave Craig a quick hug and slid onto her bunk. Giving him a cheerful grin, she made a shooing motion with her hands. "I'll be fine. Hurry." Then she tucked her hands under her to pretend they were still tied.

Craig stiffened as the thud of footsteps sounded on the steps to the porch and he moved swiftly across the room to his bunk, where he positioned himself.

The words came more clearly now.

"We wouldn't have to do anything with them, if you two hadn't flubbed up," Jerry Pratty said contemptuously, which brought on another round of arguing.

"You sure didn't mind my help findin' you a nice hidey hole to stay in," Freddy Pratty snapped back at him.

The footsteps and voices stopped abruptly on the porch and they heard the senior Pratty's angry voice again. "I thought I told you to lock this door."

"I did lock it," came the equally angry reply from his son.

"Well, if you locked it, where's the lock?"

"Shut up, Freddy."

"*Uncle* Fred to you, Pretty Boy."

"If they're gone, there'll be hell to pay." Jerry's cold tight words were spoken precisely.

"He ain't goin' nowhere. I tied him wicked tight and if she got loose, it weren't me that tied her."

Sylvia could imagine the calculated freezing look that Jerry would give Freddy over that statement. Then she heard the doorknob turn and the door was shoved so violently backward that the knob hit the wall and bounced the door back. I hope it didn't hit Jody, she thought, not daring to look in that direction.

A cautious foot nudged the door open again. The dim light streaking from the board slits and the open doorway showed the outline of still bodies in the bunks, lulling the Prattys into the room while they continued their arguing.

"I still say we take the woman with us." Roy chuckled and the sound sent a chill through Sylvia. "She could be our hostage to Mexico."

"That's kidnapping, stupid."

"Dad, get him off my back or I'll . . ."

"You and who else, Pretty Boy?"

"Stop it!"

The razor sharp command whipped through the room, demanding instant silence. No one moved for a moment, then Roy, apparently encouraged by Freddy's stillness, advanced to Sylvia's bunk. He dusted off a spot on the edge and sat next to her, his gun still firmly clasped in his hand.

"Hello, Miss Prim and Proper Perkins." He smirked at her.

Sylvia stared steadily back at him, trying not to let her pounding heart betray her increasing tension, willing her arms to stay put behind her back instead of scratching out his eyes.

How had she ever thought him handsome? His face as it hovered over hers had to be the ugliest of God's creations. She closed her eyes to shut out his gloating countenance. *How much longer, Craig?* When Roy reached out his long fingers and caressed her cheek, Sylvia couldn't suppress a shudder and a rush of anger. The toad! She whipped her head around and crunched down hard on his finger.

Roy screamed as he jumped up from the bunk, dropped his gun and grabbed his finger with the other hand.

Before Roy could recover from the surprise and agony of her attack, Craig flipped out of his bunk and hurled himself across the room. Sylvia scrambled to a sitting position and grabbed the gun.

When Craig launched himself across the room, Freddy whirled with his gun pointed toward the two struggling figures. At that moment, Jody kicked the door shut, darkening the room further. Under the dim cover, he twisted the gun from Freddy's hand before the hatted man knew another person was there, and smashed his fist into Freddy's stomach.

A defeated Freddy folded to his feet in slow motion as Sylvia watched in fascination. He actually crumpled. Just like in the movies.

"Don't do it, Pratty."

Richard's voice sounded so authoritative, Sylvia thought, as he stepped out of the kitchen and sighted down his gun barrel at Jerry.

The only Pratty left in working condition glanced from where Richard was casually leaning against the kitchen doorway to the gun in Jody's hands and the bunk where Roy stood perfectly still. He held his gun defiantly against Richard, betraying not a whit of passion when Sylvia clicked off the safety of Roy's confiscated weapon and pointed it directly at him.

Jerry waved his gun back and forth, "You may have three guns, but I have an advantage you don't."

"And what is that, Pratty?" Craig asked as Sylvia slid off the bunk to stand beside him, and Richard slowly moved forward.

"You won't shoot me." He hurled the words at them and pivoted towards Richard.

Richard fell to the floor seconds before the crashing sound of a discharging gun roared in the room and Sylvia cried out in despair at her fallen friend. Jerry yanked open the door and dashed outside, his desperate footsteps pounding across the porch.

"Take this one." Craig shoved a wilted Roy at Jody.

"Gladly." Jody grimly forced him onto the floor beside Freddy, holding Freddy's own gun on them.

As Craig started out the door after Jerry, a loud splintering sound and a screech came from outside just as Richard rolled up from the floor and followed him. *He's not dead. Thank you, God.* But before Sylvia could allow herself the luxury of relief, she had to know what was going on outside.

Handing the deadly weapon to Jody as he stood guard over the two men on the floor, she warily stepped around them and went to the door to view the scene outside.

The top step held a wretched Jerry captive by the right knee. In his frantic haste he had stepped squarely on the decayed wood and it had split, caving in and taking him with it. The upper half of his body was sprawled down the other steps, his gun flung several feet from the reach of his hand. It seemed to Sylvia that she could see the mist of his dreams escaping from him and vanishing into the forest. As his dreams died he seemed to shrivel visibly and she almost felt sorry for him. Almost.

With Craig's direction, the Prattys were soon tied up with their own ropes and loaded into the back of their truck. Poking her head into the front of the truck, Sylvia found the rusty metal box and the camouflaged gold bars tucked on the floor in a cardboard box.

"Sylvia, can you drive this thing?" Craig asked.

"If I can drive Jody's old truck, I can drive anything," she answered, ignoring her brother's indignant remark and hopping into the cab. Craig, Richard and Jody climbed into the back of the truck to watch their captives.

Thinking that it was much better to be the captors than the captives, Sylvia revved up the engine and moved the gears into place. Turning jerkily around in the clearing, she headed back down the logging road.

She bounced along, glancing often in the mirror to check on the men, and finally came to a main road that she recognized. It wasn't long before she was pulling up before the sheriff's office. The amazement on Sheriff Maab's skinny face when Richard brought him out to view their captives and Craig explained who they were made Sylvia's day. Then the sheriff turned all business and, calling a couple of deputies, he took the Prattys off their hands and into the county jail until they could be transferred elsewhere.

Craig wanted nothing more than to be with Sylvia, but his job wasn't quite over yet. He needed to fully explain the situation to the sheriff and to call his current employers to let them know their money had been recovered—and to cancel his term of employment. Only after this was done could he take the time to talk to Sylvia.

"Is your truck around, Jody?"

"Sure, why?"

"I want you to take Sylvia home for me. I'll be here a little longer."

"Can't I stay with you?" Sylvia asked, then could have bitten off her tongue at the begging words. She pinched her bottom lip with her teeth and avoided Craig's eyes, so she missed the softness in his gaze as he answered.

"I'll drop by your house for a few minutes after I'm done here. Okay?"

"Sure." She turned and walked away from everyone.

Jody came pounding down the sidewalk after her. "Wait a minute, Sis. Old Bertha's over on the next street."

"So?" she said, keeping up the swift pace until they reached the corner. Then she turned to face him.

"Now, would you like to tell me why we raced two blocks out of the way?" Jody shoved his hands into his pockets and waited.

"Don't, Jody." Her strained voice sounded harsh even to herself.

"Hey, Sylvia. It's all over. You can relax now." Jody sought to reassure her and was appalled at the depth of misery in the look she gave him.

"That's just it. It's all over now and Craig will go away."

A low whistle escaped Jody's lips. "So you guys weren't just putting on a show back in the camp. You got it bad, girl."

"Don't I know it." She drew her sleeve roughly across her face and caught back a sob. "Take me home, Jody."

They trailed around the block to Bertha in dreary silence. As if sensing their mood, the truck started immediately and gave as near to a purr as she could, chugging down the streets of Devon to Sylvia's sanctuary.

When they pulled to the curb in front of her house Jody walked her to the door and inside without a word, then he hugged her tightly. "Can I do anything?"

"No." Sylvia tried to smile at him.

"Want me to stay?"

"No, I want to be alone now." She waited until he had passed her and was reaching for the door. "Jody."

When he paused, she took a deep breath and confessed, "I'm going with him—if he'll have me."

Jody looked back at her face, her eyes, all asking him to understand, to support her. Reaching out, he took a handful of her hair, tugged on it, and grinned. "Go for it, Sis."

The smile started tiny, then grew until she looked like Sylvia again, not a forlorn waif. "Thanks, Brother." She blew him a kiss as he backed out the door, still grinning at her.

The thud and click of the door sounded final to Sylvia. Was she being hasty? Craig had given her no sign that he wanted her to go with him. Standing in the middle of her living room, she felt a tender smile hover on her lips as she gazed at the old-fashioned sofa.

There they had shared the excitement over finding the key. Wandering through the kitchen, her eye caught on the innocent looking wood box and she remembered the fear—and fun—they had had escaping down the elevator. She turned slowly, gazing at the beloved furnishings and strolling through the downstairs of her house, seeing Craig in every corner. Finally she ended back in the living room, wondering at how empty her house seemed without Craig in it. Whatever happened to old self-sufficient Sylvia?

Just thinking about him leaving left her with an empty feeling. Yes, the house was lovely and her things were lovely, and her job offered the compensation of knowing she was touching lives, but things were just things. *That mammoth has worked his way right into your heart and life.* Sylvia snorted. *With-*

out Craig I'll be as lonely and empty as my big house feels.

A rush of elation sped through her as she knew that she was making the right decision because she belonged with Craig. Suddenly she couldn't wait until he came.

During the next hour Sylvia thought she would surely wear a path right through the rug into the hardwood floors underneath. She changed her mind about going with Craig five times and compensated for her nervousness by constantly checking out the front window.

Her drapes were in dire danger of being shredded by her nervous fingers when she finally spied Craig striding up her walk. A quick knock sounded on the door, but Sylvia froze by the window, unable to answer it. What if he didn't want her to go with him?

The door opened and Craig called to her. Still no answer would come from her throat. She threaded her fingers in the pull cord without thinking and tugged on it. The drapes swished wide open and the rays of the late afternoon sun spilled in, enveloping Sylvia in a cocoon of warmth.

Waiting by the window, she saw Craig as a huge shadow looming in the doorway. No menace or threat emanated from his presence, only a sense of uncertainty, of which Sylvia already had plenty.

"Sylvia?"

Their voices sounded simultaneously: "We need to talk." After a faint smile from Sylvia and a low chuckle from Craig, he gestured to her to go first.

Swallowing hard, she managed to ingest her pride and, reaching out, she took one of his hands and held it lightly with both her own. "Craig, I don't want you to leave me here. I want to go with you and be your lover." Her green eyes searched his face for an answer.

Craig touched her cheek in a gentle gesture and smiled intimately down at her. Her breath came faster. He was going to say yes!

"No, Sylvia. I—"

The bright sunlight was no longer a warm cocoon, but a smothering blanket over an iced stone. Sylvia felt cold and alone and naked in the world for all to see. Turning away from the light into the depths of the living room, so that he could not see her face, she mustered up the last shreds of her pride. "So...it's been fun...good—"

Strong arms stopped her and held her. Craig's hand slipped over her mouth and shut off her choked syllables, and he turned her around to face him. She stared blankly at him, hearing nothing, feeling nothing.

"Don't look at me like that, Sylvia." He shook her lightly. "Didn't you hear me? I've decided I want to live in a small town with a white picket fence, two-point-five children—and a red-headed amazon for a wife." His smile was as warm as the afternoon sun streaming through the windows.

The words vibrated loudly in the room, lingering and caressing and penetrating Sylvia's mind. Her eyes widened, going from blank to sparkling. "You do! Well, there's no accounting for tastes." And she threw herself into Craig's arms, right in front of the bay window.

He cradled her, rocking her from side to side as she alternately laughed and cried on his chest, all the while her hands clasped in a painful grip behind his back as if she would never, ever let him go. When her hysterics subsided, Sylvia looked up at Craig's face. Releasing her hands, she traced his jawbone, up and over his ear and behind his head, sinking her hands into his wealth of dark hair.

"There's also a reward for finding the money," Craig said softly.

"Wonderful. I'll give my part to Jody. He can start his own business."

"I think I'll give my part to Aunt Willy." Craig smiled down at her.

No more words were needed between them. Craig took her mouth gently at first, then the driving hunger between them flared and he demanded entrance. She opened and felt his moist tongue seeking, dancing, unleashing her needs. Standing on tiptoe, Sylvia kissed him back with all the pent-up energy the resolved excitement and tension had released in her.

"Mmm, why don't we continue this discussion upstairs?" Craig asked softly, smiling down at her, his dark eyes glowing.

At that exact moment a shrill whistle came from the sidewalk outside the window. "Wow! Miz Perkins," a young voice shouted. "When's the wedding?"

Sylvia rolled her eyes and looked out to see Jimmy Johnston standing over his fallen bike, a delighted look on his adolescent face.

Craig leaned over and yelled out the opened casement. "Next week! Want to be an usher?"

"Yeah!" He was on his ten-speed in seconds. "I gotta tell this. The kids'll never believe me." He pedaled off furiously and yelled back at them. "I'll be back later."

"Now look what you've done." Sylvia looked at Craig sternly.

"What?" He tried to look properly chastened.

"Now we'll have to have my entire senior class involved so no one will feel left out."

"No problem. Now, where were we?" His eyes gleamed at her as he swooped down again.

She stepped back and shook her finger at him. "And we'll never be able to get married in one week."

"So make it two." He reached for her again.

A flicker in the window across the street registered in the corner of Sylvia's eyes and she began to giggle.

A resigned look crossed Craig's face. "Now what?"

Sylvia pointed.

"Is Mrs. Whatchamacallher watching again?"

She nodded. "It's Mrs. Winegath and, yes, she is."

A glint of wickedness flashed into Craig's eyes. "Then let's give her something to talk about." He scooped Sylvia up in his arms and threw her to the floor, pouncing on top of her in full view of the window. While they remained together on the floor, he grabbed the shade cord and pulled, sending the drapes sliding across in front of their nosy neighbor's view.

"That'll kill her," Sylvia said, chuckling.

The chuckles stopped as she found their new position just as suggestive in feeling as in viewing. Apparently Craig felt the same way because he rolled off her with a groan and clasped his hands to his head. "It's gonna kill me to wait two weeks."

But it didn't.

Two weeks later, after frantic activity of the entire Perkins clan, the wedding that half of Devon had been waiting ten years for took place, and Sylvia Marie Perkins became Sylvia Perkins McDonald. Her excited senior class did indeed participate as ushers and maids of honor.

"Never was there a lovelier bride," was the whisper of the congregation, as Sylvia glided down the aisle, even though covetous eyes stole often to the tall, rugged man waiting beside the altar with an impatient look on his handsome face.

But no one was happier than Momma and Aunt Willy as they dried their tears together and smiled at the success of their schemes to get a man for Sylvia.